Melting Pot of Narratives

Tales from the Indian Subcontinent

Dr Anagha Keskar

Ukiyoto Publishing

All global publishing rights are held by

Ukiyoto Publishing

Published in 2024

Content Copyright © Dr Anagha Keskar

ISBN 9789364947060

All rights reserved.

No part of this publication may be reproduced, transmitted, or stored in a retrieval system, in any form by any means, electronic, mechanical, photocopying, recording or otherwise, without the prior permission of the publisher.

The moral rights of the author have been asserted.

This is a work of fiction. Names, characters, businesses, places, events, locales, and incidents are either the products of the author's imagination or used in a fictitious manner. Any resemblance to actual persons, living or dead, or actual events is purely coincidental.

This book is sold subject to the condition that it shall not by way of trade or otherwise, be lent, resold, hired out or otherwise circulated, without the publisher's prior consent, in any form of binding or cover other than that in which it is published.

www.ukiyoto.com

Kalpana, Priti, Lata and Sangeeta,
Now with these stories translated especially for you and others like you who love stories, there is no more excuse not to read them.

Contents

Chip and the Old Block	1
Double-Check	31
Generation Gap	51
Lessons Unlearned	77
Relieved	91
The Other Side of the Table	139
The Promise	160
The Religion	177
About the Author	*203*

Chip and the Old Block

Before entering the room, Pratap stood at the door and peeped inside. An open book was kept on the table and Bapukaka was looking at the beautiful mango tree from the window. He was watching a numerous green shades spread beyond the tree.

He entered the room.

"Daddy, I wish to talk to you." said Pratap with head bowed down.

"Come, sit down," Bapukaka replied warmly, meeting Pratap's gaze with a steady look.

"I have something to tell you," Pratap repeated his earlier statement.

Bapukaka reached for a homemade bookmark from the pen-stand on his table, carefully marking the page in his book before closing it.

"Now tell me what's on your mind," said Bapukaka, his eyes fixed on Pratap with an expectant look. Pratap avoided direct eye contact, shifting his gaze to the front page of the book. There, in green ink, he read the title: 'Rural Development: Concept & Reality'. Unconsciously, he swallowed hard.

"Are you angry with me? I've noticed a change in your demeanor since I arrived..."

"No, not at all. Why would I be angry?" Bapukaka replied calmly.

"I'm not the only one who senses your resentment. Everyone has picked up on it. Patil uncle, Krishna Aunty, and Shrikant; they've all noticed," Pratap continued.

"What have they noticed? Do they think I'm annoyed?" Bapukaka inquired.

"Not exactly, but you're not your usual self. You hardly engage in conversation," Pratap explained.

""When a person is deeply absorbed in their work, it's natural for them to be in a contemplative mood. They get lost in their thoughts and memories. You all are unnecessarily misinterpreting things," Bapukaka responded.

"It's not just about not talking to us; why are you planning to move to Pimpalwadi?" Pratap persisted.

"That was bound to happen sooner or later. Do you think my decision to leave this place has anything to do with your decision? Are you out of your mind?" Bapukaka retorted.

"Daddy, you're growing tired with age. I thought you were quite content here. Now that Mom is no longer with you, why are you considering starting anew in a different place? How much longer do you plan to live this nomadic life? The moment I decided to go abroad, you started dismantling our home. Daddy, I couldn't follow in Mom's and your footsteps. Why don't you try to understand me?" Pratap explained earnestly.

"It's not what you think. I've come to terms with the fact that you can't follow the same path as us. I'm not upset with you at all. You have your own perspectives and beliefs, and I respect your individuality. My decision to move has nothing to do with your decision to emigrate. I had already begun planning this move long before that. Since you were preoccupied with your own plans, you didn't notice it. The young leaders and social workers of Pimpalwadi approached me last year. They've been urging me to relocate there. Nana Thakar is well-informed about our organizations here. I spent six months training him further."

"Is it absolutely necessary to leave this town?" Pratap questioned. "You're comfortable here. Everything is settled. If I hadn't decided to go to Atlanta, would you still be moving to Pimpalwadi so soon?"

Bapukaka extended his arm to retrieve a brownish file from the top of the cupboard. Opening it, he searched until he found what he sought, then handed the open file to Pratap. Placing his index finger on the top right corner of the paper, he said, "Now, look at this date: September 1997. I requested Mr. Shelar from Pimpalwadi to give me a six-month period to wind things up."

"I cannot come to terms with it. There's a persistent ache at the bottom of my heart. I would have preferred if you had bombarded me with accusations or scolded me, even fought with me. At least then I would have had the chance to present my side and argue with you."

"What would be the point? I already know your arguments. You'll repeat what I've heard from your justifications time and again. 'In the USA, there's ample opportunity. They respect individuals based on their work, not their position, caste, or class. It's challenging to work in a corrupt environment, with dirty politics, inefficient governance, corruption, illiteracy, and superstitions.' What else is there to add?"

"Isn't it all true? Every word rings true, and you've experienced it firsthand. In fact, few have witnessed these malpractices as closely as you have."

"If that's the case, why waste your time trying to convince me? I never asked you to change your plans. Whatever lessons or wisdom I wanted to impart, I've already shared with you, and countless others. I have nothing more to say. You're a wise individual. You've observed our lives and those of others up close. You have every right to disagree with me. Nobody is absolutely right or wrong. There will always be differences of opinion."

"I know you say you are not angry but you don't share your daily experiences with me as before. I feel the distance and the indifference."

"Well, what do you want me to do? If one wishes to avoid getting annoyed, they must resign themselves from it. How can I blame you? My father sent me to Britain so that I could complete F R C S. Actually, he couldn't afford it. He literally had to starve so that I could finish the course. He had magnificent dreams for me. What did I do? I couldn't fulfill any of his dreams. I neither completed the course nor set up a successful medical practice. In my mother's words, my dreams were like those of a beggar. I did what I believed was right, what I wanted to do. Today, it's your turn to tailor your life according to your dreams. I have no right to contradict you."

"Dad, please believe me. If I were not convinced that my career can only be strengthened in the USA, I would not have thought of deserting you and my country. I am not after money and the life it offers."

"I know it. But even if anybody decides to emigrate for monetary gains, who are we to question its desirability? It could be his philosophy of life. It could be compatible with his mind-set."

At that moment, Patil uncle and four other people from their town came to meet with Bapukaka, interrupting the conversation between father and son. As he left the room, Pratap could hear Baban pleading with Bapukaka to cancel his plan and stay back.

"Bapukaka, please don't leave us. We were mistaken, blinded by our own biases. You tried your best to convince us about the development plans, and now the whole town stands behind you. Why leave us now?"

Pratap didn't wait to hear Bapukaka's reply. He knew what it could be. He could recollect it word by word. Bapukaka used to say,

"I am not angry with you. You know what measures should be taken for the development of your town. You have resolved all the differences among yourselves. The youth of the town and even the ladies have come together for a common cause. Anana, Tatya, Bhau, Pirya, and many others have assumed leadership. My share of work is over. You do not need me now. Eight years back, you were novices in the field and were struggling. Some other such stragglers need me now."

That was the conversation between him and the people of Babhulgaon when he left for Chandgaon, and with the people of Chandgaon while shifting from Chandgaon to Udgaon.

Bapukaka engaged in conversation with the local leaders for some time but remained firm on his decision.

Upon returning to the kitchen for lunch, he found Pratap surrounded by heaps of papers, with the wooden cupboard left ajar as he sorted through them. Hearing Bapukaka's footsteps, he glanced up, his eyes catching sight of Bapukaka. Pratap was holding a photograph featuring Bapukaka and his late mother, Sushila. His eyes glistened with unshed tears, filled with nostalgia.

Observing Pratap's emotional state, Bapukaka gently inquired, "Pratap, what are you doing?"

"These are my old school books, notebooks, and the prizes I received in school. Mom kept all these things. Now, it seems meaningless to hold onto them, especially since you'll be moving from place to place." replied Pratap.

"You can set aside whatever you wish to keep and discard the rest. But let's have lunch first. We can discuss it further over food."

As they began their meal, Pratap continued,

"Dad, I admire your dedication to social work, but I can't shake off one thing from my mind. Mom had to endure a lot because of your stubbornness. She had to constantly relocate from one place to another. I understand your passion for social causes, but perhaps you could have stayed in one place. Your efforts would have been more widely recognized if you had remained dedicated to a single organization. You could have garnered appreciation from political leaders and the government, perhaps even received awards. But you chose to move around as you pleased, and Mom had to comply without protest. She had to rebuild our home and forge new relationships each time. I don't know how she managed it. I doubt I could ever emulate her strength and resilience."

"She never insisted that you should behave like her. One of your statements is wrong."

"What's wrong? Is it wrong to aspire for a simple, common man's life? I cannot spend my whole life in selfless social work. But I will do everything in my capacity to mobilize resources for your social activities. Every activity demands resources. Don't forget that."

"You have misunderstood my words. I did not mean to say that your choice of lifestyle is wrong. You mentioned that Mom accepted my nomadic life at my insistence. I was referring to that statement."

"What is wrong there? She must have cherished some dreams and aspired for a better, affluent life. She must have desired a tiny house of her own. She may have hoped for her physician husband to establish a practice and provide her with a prosperous living. Let alone these things; she definitely did not want her only son to be away for schooling just because there was no school in the vicinity."

"It is quite possible. She must have had some rosy dreams. But she never uttered a word indicating those dreams. I had explained to her what I wanted in life before our wedding. She accepted my aims and objectives wholeheartedly. And let me tell you one thing: she was instrumental in our nomadic life. She wanted it. Just now you were talking about social and political recognition and awards. I was tempted by these superfluous things, not she. It was her idea that we should move from place to place. She made me promise that I will continue to lead this nomadic life even after her demise."

"What are you talking about? Her insistence and promise to you? I can't believe it."

"That is a fact. Shall I ever tell lies?"

"Even if it were true, how long are you going to move in search of a new home at intervals? You are aging and getting frail."

"I will continue this lifestyle until I leave this field. When it becomes impossible for me to work, I will come and make a home with you, wherever you happen to stay. Shall I serve you some vegetables? You're not eating anything."

"I am eating, Dad. Serve me a spoonful, and you finish the rest."

Bapukaka served the vegetable to Pratap and finished the remaining. He said, 'You don't seem to believe that Sushila was instrumental in my decision to move from one place to another."

"How can I believe it? I've seen her dedicating her life to your aspirations, aims, and social service. I've seen you declaring your plan to move and her winding up things without uttering a word of protest."

"What you've observed is true, but you don't know the reasons behind it. You really have no idea what type of woman your Mom was. That time we were stationed in Jambhulgaon. You were very young. We had conducted a health camp. Bhausaheb Pawar had come for the inauguration ceremony. He openly praised me and my social activities in the huge gathering. I felt elated. Ten years of my medical practice and social work were rightfully recognized. That was when Sushila and I had a serious argument. She did not approve of my work and the systems I had meticulously established in our organizations. She bluntly criticized me."

Pratap glanced at his Dad while Bapukaka continued.

"You are right. She always helped the cause I stood for. She undertook complementary activities like uplifting rural women. She believed that since women constitute fifty percent of the population, no social worker should neglect womenfolk. I used to charge meager fees for the patients. Half the patients did not pay a penny. She never complained about it. Now that you are grown up, I do not mind telling you one very personal thing. She longed for a daughter but for the sake of social work, we decided not to have another child. She agreed to it for my sake."

"Then what was it that she did not approve?"

"I was receiving recognition and being felicitated as a sincere social worker. She thought that it had an adverse effect on my work. She said that I was gradually becoming self-righteous. She was worried that I myself was turning into an egotist about my clean and transparent financial dealings. She thought I was getting intoxicated because of the compliments I used to receive from all quarters."

"My God! Did she say so overtly?"

"For the last many years, I have been writing a diary. You know it. After finishing lunch, I will give you my diary. You can go through it."

"I do not doubt your statement. If you feel awkward to let me share your intimate personal things, don't bother."

"We did not have a private life. We had thrown all the facts openly before the world. You will see how a capable woman can keep a hold on her husband if she means. I have read those pages of my diary umpteen times. Whenever I am skeptical about my social behavior I read those pages. Our heated arguments, discussions, and my opinions about the whole issue are meticulously written."

"Is that so? Then I'll certainly take a look at it. You can give me the diary, and I'll read it once I'm done decluttering these papers."

"Take your time."

"A moment ago, I mentioned my plan to send money from the USA; that's precisely what I intend to do. I'll organize migrated Indians into small groups and encourage them to raise resources. They likely feel some sense of obligation toward the motherland. I'll approach them systematically, perhaps through websites. Why do you find it amusing?"

"You've inadvertently adopted our language of organizing people. It amuses me."

"I'm serious about it, though. I genuinely mean to follow through."

"That will certainly make my work easier."

....

Pratap opened Bapukaka's gray-colored diary. There were no daily entries; instead, Bapukaka had recorded only significant events.

Bapukaka had placed a bookmark at the relevant pages. Pratap removed the bookmark and began reading Bapukaka's bold handwriting on the yellowed pages of the diary.

Date: March 9, 1969

Today, during his public address, Bhausaheb praised my efforts and contributions. The mayor and other members of the social volunteer group also commended my work. Additionally, youths from nearby towns such as Kelgaon and Bhambrewadi presented garlands as a token of appreciation. There was mention of the possibility of my nomination for a prestigious title. After overcoming numerous obstacles and persevering diligently, I now feel a deep sense of satisfaction and fulfillment with this accomplishment.

A decade ago, I engaged in a heated argument with my parents and left home with just a single trunk. Naturally, they were deeply upset by my decision. I vividly recall that day. I arrived at a modest single room in Mr. Inamdar's mansion. Although the townsfolk were aware of the arrival of a new doctor, they seemed hesitant to approach me. It appeared that they did not consider me as one of their own. Until then, they had never sought medical advice for common ailments like coughs, colds, and fevers.

The members of the Inamdar family were incredibly warm and welcoming towards me, treating me as one of their own. Nana Inamdar, in particular, would engage in lengthy conversations with me regularly. Despite my daily cooking routine, he insisted on inviting me for lunch and dinner frequently. Although he respected and held me in high regard, he harbored reservations about my decision to forgo completing the F R C S course in England and my subsequent rift with my parents. However, upon learning of my broader intentions to extend my activities beyond medical practice and contribute to the socioeconomic transformation of rural society, he expressed his approval. Together with Rajabhau, I conducted experiments on the farm, established a library for the literate individuals, and sponsored the training of several youths in agriculture, covering their expenses in the process.

Despite the initial hesitancy, when a cholera epidemic struck the town and there was no Primary Health Center available, the common people had no alternative but to seek my assistance. This dire situation compelled them to overcome their reservations and approach me for help. As they faced the pressing need for medical aid, they gradually began to place their trust in me.

We managed to construct a humble dispensary building through collective contributions from the community. Over time, this structure was expanded with the addition of three rooms, transforming it into a makeshift hospital. Local youths were trained to educate the populace on healthy dietary practices, water sanitation, and hygiene. Inspired by our efforts, Sable teacher enlisted Prakash Dhakne to create visually striking posters, which were prominently displayed in the market and along the main thoroughfare. Traditionally, Bhagabai and Shevanta served as midwives in the town, albeit without formal training. I took it upon myself to provide them with training and equipped them with a first aid kit. Despite initial skepticism and attempts to impede our progress, the gradual yet tangible improvements in the community silenced detractors and skeptics.

Following our marriage, Sushila brought a newfound energy to our endeavors. She took the initiative to organize women and educate them on basic aspects of daily life. Our movement gained momentum, catching the attention of government officials at the district level, who began informing us about various government schemes and campaigns. As a result, wells were dug, percolation tanks were constructed, and efforts were made towards afforestation on unused land and closed public pastures. Additionally, a public dairy was established, followed by a milk collection center. I personally ensured meticulous oversight of public funds, fostering trust and confidence among the community. Subsequently, international organizations extended financial assistance, further bolstering people's confidence in our initiatives.

The neighboring villages observed these developments keenly, harboring similar aspirations for progress but lacking dynamic leadership. They found themselves emulating our initiatives and sought my advice, elevating my name to the forefront of their discussions. It became common parlance that "nothing will happen without Bapu's advice." Over time, significant advancements were made: electricity was introduced, bio gas units were installed, hospitals and permanent roads were constructed, and prayer houses with spacious community halls were established. Additionally, cooperative dairies and pilot projects for vegetable and fruit farming were initiated, necessitating the introduction of truck and tempo services, as well as the emergence of retailers and shops. Today's celebration is a testament to these collective efforts. People continue to seek my counsel, believing that "nothing is possible unless Bapu looks into it," a sentiment that brings me immense satisfaction.

I have sacrificed everything for my country and my people, and this sacrifice hasn't gone unnoticed. The people are fully aware of my efforts and they express their gratitude openly. Even my parents, who initially protested against my decisions, have now embraced my path. Seeing my photograph in newspapers or catching glimpses of me on TV or radio fills them with pride. While I may not have fulfilled their wishes for big cars and an affluent lifestyle, the sight of me living in a fairly good house and hosting dignitaries in my drawing room brings them a sense of blessing.

Date: 10th March 1969

Yesterday was a significant day for me. It's a pity that Sushila chose to argue with me on that very day. Most other women in her position would have been delighted and would have appreciated their husband's achievements. But Sushila is different! She doesn't appreciate the value in ceremonies, photo sessions, visitors, and dignitaries. I don't understand why.

Why was she upset with me? Is she jealous of my success? She has been equally involved in all my social activities from day one, and I don't deny it. And yet, I'm the one who receives all the credit. Could this be the reason behind her strange behavior?

Yesterday, everyone was congratulating me at the lunch table, but she didn't seem as enthusiastic as she usually is. I thought she must be under work pressure, having to look after hundreds of guests. However, she seemed to be sulking even when we were alone after the program. I couldn't help but ask her what the matter was.

"Are you not feeling well?" I asked.

"Who says so? What can happen to me? I am fine," she curtly replied.

"Did anybody offend you?"

"Not at all. I am the wife of Bapu, the great social worker! Who would dare to offend me? All the people are showering you with compliments. Nothing moves unless you wish it moved," she said, her tone tinged with sarcasm. I was annoyed.

"They just stated the fact. Are you sorry about it?" I asked.

"I am sorry for that. But you are misinterpreting my remark. It is not what you intend to imply," she said in an aggressive tone.

I was taken aback.

"You admit that you feel sorry, right? Shall I then surmise that you are jealous of me?"

"No, I am not jealous. But I pity you and I am afraid," she replied.

I was utterly disappointed by her weird behavior. If one's dear ones behave in this fashion, what else could be one's reaction? Inadvertently, I raised my voice.

"You feel pity for me? And what are you afraid of?"

"I will answer your question only if you promise not to shout at me," she calmly said.

I was nonplussed. I glared at her with rage. She kept staring at me without blinking her eyelids.

"I won't raise my voice. Are you satisfied? Now will you answer my question?"

"Is it a gentleman's word, a promise? Are you going to listen quietly and calmly?"

I kept quiet for a few seconds. She did not utter a word.

"I am listening. Now proceed and speak out."

"These ceremonies and programmes will chop off your wings. They tempt a person and it is bad for any individual. There is one funny thing about excessive praise. Till the time one listens to it, one is amply aware of one's capability. But the moment you listen to it and keep on listening to it often one starts overestimating oneself. One feels greater than what he really is. When everybody starts offering compliments, the person starts believing in his magnified greatness," she replied unperturbed.

"What do you mean? Whatever was said about me was false? Do you think that inflated my ego and made me excessively conceited?"

"This has not happened till now. It may become a reality if this continues to happen often. You know the stories of meditating sages from our Hindu mythology who aspired for revelation of God. They used to be distracted by the Gods by bestowing upon them some supernatural powers. Once the sages were lured by those powers they were inclined to forget their initial aspirations. These programmes serve the same purpose. They distract one's attention from the prime aim and core field. That is why I am worried."

"Thank God, you admit that I deserve all the words of praise. I don't understand anything about your babbling about excessive conceit."

"Most of what they said in those speeches was true; but not each and every word. You try to recollect. The initial plan of Cooperative Dairy was put forth by Sakharam. You opposed it because you thought it to be impractical. He talked to you, convinced you that it could be materialized. He implemented the plan successfully from A to Z. We both are witness to it. Nobody uttered his name in his speech. He should have been given due credit."

"Today the dairy is standing on a formidable base because of me. I gave it a strong organizational frame. So what's wrong if they mention my name?

Sushila chuckled.

I asked her, "Why are you chuckling?"

"Sakharam was with you all the time. He has worked hard for it. Why didn't you give him some important post in the dairy? What would have happened if you had stayed behind the scene? Sakharam is not as educated as you, but he is intelligent and dependable. He has inborn leadership qualities. Why do you want to be at the forefront?"

"Are you referring to the Women's Cottage Industry?"

"I'm not singling out any particular organization. This applies to every initiative we undertake. Consider the women's cottage industry and the literacy program led by Shanta and Pushpa. I support them, but I ensure they receive full recognition for their efforts. Why do you insist on being credited as president or advisor in every organization? Shouldn't we entrust full responsibility to those directly involved? After all, they're the ones managing every aspect of the activity."

"What exactly are you suggesting? That I take credit without contributing anything? Let's not overlook the fact that the funding we receive is largely because of my reputation and influence."

"I understand your perspective. Let me clarify; it's not just about 'you', but all of us benefiting from the funding. Until now, I haven't voiced any objection to your name being associated with our organizations and village for their betterment. However, I see things evolving. If the organization's name is exploited solely to enhance personal reputation, I won't stand for it, even if that person happens to be my husband. My concern isn't solely about taking credit; it's about fostering independence among the people. That's the crux of the matter."

"I understand your concern about the self-confidence of others. However, if I solely delegate responsibility to subordinates, the organization may not function as smoothly. It's essential to strike a balance between empowering others and ensuring effective management. That's the challenge."

Sushila smiled again, and I completely lost my composure. Without thinking, I grabbed a book from the table and hurled it at her.

"Why are you smiling like a fool all the time?" I shouted in frustration.

"Raising your voice won't make your statement true. You're not accustomed to anyone challenging you. Whenever you decide something, everyone is expected to comply silently. You argue that people lack self-confidence. But have you ever considered why they lack it?"

"Alright, I haven't considered it. Since you seem to have all the answers, why don't you enlighten me? Or are you suggesting that I'm the one responsible for undermining their self-confidence? I won't accept that. I've taught them everything, educated them in numerous ways, and helped them realize their potential and hidden talents. Are you unwilling to acknowledge this?"

"I completely agree with you. You trained them and facilitated their growth. But please don't get upset; you never allowed them to surpass you. Allow them to make decisions, allow them to make mistakes. If their decision turns out to be wrong, guide them back on the right path. They will learn from their mistakes. If they are right, encourage them with praise."

"This is public money. Their mistakes may cause a set back to the work. The organization would have to pay enormous price for it."

"Indeed, setbacks can serve as valuable lessons for future growth and independence. Embracing these challenges and learning from them can foster resilience and self-reliance among the team members, ultimately leading to stronger and more sustainable progress for the organization." said Sushila.

"Without my support?"

"What's wrong? Are you shocked? Shouldn't anybody grow without you? What would you say about Maruti? Doesn't he have confidence? He seeks your advice out of respect, more to please you than to genuinely seek guidance. Won't he be able to run the school without your guidance? Didn't he prepare the whole proposal for secondary school single handed? He dealt with the concerned Government officers. He kept the ball rolling. You would have been offended had he not told you every detail beforehand. That is why he consults you."

"Do you really feel that I am curbing Maruti's prospects? Are you bent upon enumerating my faults?"

"That's not the case. I am fully aware of your qualities and your capability. Nobody knows it better than me. You have much more potential than what was said yesterday. But I would not like anyone to portray you like a super God and thereby weaken you. I will not like if anyone uses you for one's political gain. Hence I resent these programmes."

She drew close, clasping my hand gently within hers, and spoke in a tender tone,"No man should consider himself greater than the organization and the principles it upholds. I believe you would concur with this sentiment. Don't confine yourself to this village. You have yet to achieve so much more."

I could see love and warmth in her eyes which I had seen many times. There was a soft pleading expression too.

Sushila ended the discussion there, redirecting the conversation to her usual daily activities. When I attempted to revisit the topic, she gently said,

"You contemplate on these points for the next four days. We can revisit this discussion on the 15th. Until then, just take some time to reflect."

March 11, 1969,

I found myself irritated with Sushila's words that day. Her remarks stung. While everyone around me praised my endeavors, she seemed unable to see my accomplishments in the same light. It wouldn't be fair to suggest she hadn't grasped my character. She's not just my wife, but my equal partner in every sense. If she feels strongly about my actions, I can't simply dismiss her concerns. She isn't like the typical woman who blindly adores her husband. Her perspective extends beyond the confines of our home.

Sushila's objections can be summarized as follows:

1. Significant portions of my time are dedicated to attending programs and receiving accolades.
2. This involvement has potentially made me self-centered and conceited.
3. I may have ceased introspecting, blindly accepting every compliment bestowed upon me.
4. I inhibit the growth of my colleagues.

5. I monopolize credit for various activities without acknowledging the hard work and merit of others.
6. Despite the presence of capable and dynamic individuals around me, I foster dependence on myself rather than empowering them.

After careful consideration, I realized that each objection raised by Sushila contained a kernel of truth. I had been so immersed in my work that I hadn't taken stock of my journey or recognized the negative patterns I had fallen into.

To summarize her disapproval

Bapu Deshpande dedicated himself tirelessly to societal betterment, driven by unwavering sincerity. However, he fell into the trap of self-righteousness, believing himself infallible. In the process, he built an empire around himself, providing a platform to wield power. Seduced by this power, he began to overshadow the very organizations and movements he sought to serve. Inadvertently, he facilitated similar behavior in others. This is a grave misstep, one from which I must liberate myself and my organizations.

Indeed, even in my private reflections, I find myself referring to public organizations as "my organizations." This reveals a dangerous tendency to possessiveness and unchecked ego. It is imperative that I rein in this inclination and cultivate humility in all aspects of my work.

March 13, 1969

Sushila remained steadfast in her decision not to revisit the topic for four days, and she remained true to her word. Her demeanor suggested that nothing out of the ordinary had occurred. Engrossed in our respective daily tasks, we carried on. However, her silence served as a catalyst for me to delve deep into introspection, analyzing my thoughts and actions with renewed scrutiny.

I'm beginning to grasp the essence of her arguments. Yesterday, Maruti presented me with a letter seeking financial aid. Upon review, I found it to be well-composed, requiring only minor corrections for spelling errors. Typically, I would have made a few alterations, perhaps tweaking a couple of sentences and adding my own insights. It wasn't to diminish Maruti's efforts, but rather a habit I'd unwittingly cultivated—believing that all correspondence must pass through my hands for final approval before being sent out. Today, however, I resisted the urge to edit the draft impulsively.

Maruti's smile was evident, a reassuring sign. We had previously collaborated on compiling a list of potential donors. He proposed that I arrange a meeting with Mr. Tolani. Instinctively, I almost consented, but I paused and responded,

"You're better equipped to handle him yourself. You have a more comprehensive understanding of the progress." Maruti readily embraced my suggestion. It dawned on me that Sushila's observations about Maruti were indeed accurate. He consistently assumed a secondary role out of respect for me.

I declared that supervising the cowsheds for a week wouldn't be feasible for me and asked Sakharam to take over. Initially hesitant, he eventually agreed after I suggested creating a detailed checklist and delegating the task to his subordinate. Now, I notice the impact of such small changes. The day after tomorrow, I will discuss with Sushila at night, and together we will chart out the future course of action.

Today's incidents have been noted down for discussion. I plan to review with her how I should handle these situations and compare it with my usual approach.

Mr. Chavan from the School Committee visited today to inquire about which social activities the school children should be involved in.

Ganu informed me that the stock of medicines intended for the facilitators needs to be replenished. He sought my decision on whether we should continue ordering from our current chemist, who has been unreasonable, or switch to another supplier.

15th March 1969

1 Sopana consulted me today regarding the cleaning of the well. He expressed concern that volunteers were hesitant to begin the routine duty of dredging the wells. It was suggested that groups be formed and provided with clear instructions regarding their responsibilities.

2 The saplings planted by the roadside are being consumed by cattle, and there is a need to replace them with fresh saplings. The question of who should manage this activity arose.

It's past 12 pm now. We had a conversation on that subject. I acknowledged that there is indeed some truth in all her allegations. It wasn't easy to admit, but I did so nonetheless. We deliberated on ways to enhance our current working style. To chart out our course of action, we resolved to meticulously document each and every incident in the coming month and then discuss potential solutions. These are the decisions we made today:

We've decided to depart from Jambhulwadi and relocate to either Chandgaon or Bhambrewadi next April, where we'll initiate similar social activities.

Before our departure, we aim to establish a robust leadership foundation in this area. As a preliminary measure, we will distribute our responsibilities among our seasoned colleagues. Over time, we'll progressively increase the workload on capable volunteers. Our focus will be on training and empowering individuals to make decisions independently.

To enhance efficiency in implementation, we plan to organize people into groups and introduce a 3/4 tier hierarchy, along with structured accountability measures.

The top-level group will be tasked with forming subordinate groups beneath them.

Following our departure from Jambhulgaon, we'll make monthly visits to oversee the ongoing work there. As time progresses, we'll gradually reduce the frequency of our visits.

On the 18th of March 1969, Sushila and I solemnly made three pledges:

1. We will always uphold the principle that the organization is greater than any individual, and society holds greater significance than the organization.
2. We commit to devising a 10-year plan for village development, with preparations to wind down our involvement in the final year.
3. We pledge to establish a model organizational structure and ensure our timely retirement, setting an example for others to follow.

We will uphold these oaths until our last day of service to society.

Both Sushila and Bapu had signed at the end of the declaration.

Pratap continued reading through the pages of the diary, absorbing the meticulous documentation of various activities, decisions, and discussions. While some of the intricate details eluded him, he couldn't help but admire the discipline and dedication evident in each entry. As he delved deeper into the diary, Pratap found himself unable to sleep well into the night. Memories of days gone by flooded his mind, with vivid images of Bapu's humble dispensary and the mango tree adorned with a circular platform in front of their home. He envisioned people gathering on the platform, seeking Bapu's counsel and guidance. Alternating with these scenes were glimpses of the primary school in Chandgaon and the serene Shiva temple in Udgaon.

He stirred awake as warm sunlight kissed his face. Bapu was already prepared to leave, Pratap noted, observing his father's readiness to depart.

He got up from the mattress. "I read the diary. Mom..." Pratap began, his voice trailing off as he processed the weight of what he had absorbed from its pages.

"I'm in a hurry. Lakhya's baby daughter is down with vomiting and loose motions. Today Dr. Kadam is not in the dispensary. Patients must be expecting me. We can talk about it later," Bapu explained, indicating the urgency of his departure.

Pratap kept gazing at Bapu's receding figure, noticing the slight droop in his shoulders and the slower pace of his gait. Each movement seemed more deliberate, perhaps a bit more feeble. A lump formed in Pratap's throat as he realized that Bapu was showing signs of aging, his once-strong frame now showing the wear and tear of time. "He's aging and getting weaker day by day," Pratap murmured to himself, a tinge of sadness in his voice.

When Bapukaka returned home, Pratap was already waiting for him, having set the table and reheated the food. Bapu washed his hands and feet, changed his sweaty clothes, and then joined Pratap at the table, where they shared the meal together.

"Dad, I read through your diary. I'd really like to read all of them. You know, I've been away in the city since my school days, so I missed out on a lot of family time with you. Whenever I came back home for vacations, you were always so busy. It made me feel like our home and our family were different from others'. I used to feel sorry and even a bit angry because I never got to spend much time with you. Even my grandparents used to criticize you for that. But after reading your diary yesterday, I finally understood the magnitude of your work. I see now what you were trying to tell me about Mom."

"So, you are convinced. I was not criticizing her."

"I understand now how Mom helped you break free from being tied down to one place. Your decision to leave here isn't just a response to my leaving. It's a natural result of your disciplined and principled life. I regret that, despite being your son and observing you closely, I couldn't inherit your dedication. I've always been drawn to urban amenities; it's just who I am, and I can't change that."

"No two individuals are alike, and that's what makes life interesting. Your path is distinct and broader than mine. I have faith that you'll apply the same passion and commitment in your own endeavors. That's all I could ask for."

"I'll be leaving next month. I'm uncertain when I'll be able to visit again and for how long. Can I ask you for a favor? Would you consider staying with me for at least a week before heading to Pimpalgaon? During that time, you'll just be my Dad, nothing else. Let me provide you with every comfort and take care of you. I'll try my best to look after you like a mother would. Will you grant me this wish for my peace of mind?"

"Are you serious?"

"You can call me crazy if you want. Please, just grant my request, and I'll feel reassured that you're not upset or disappointed with my decision."

"Alright, we'll go next week. Are you satisfied now?"

"Thank you, Dad. Thank you for everything."

Double-Check

15th June 2035. The scorching heat of Delhi made it impossible to gaze at the bright sunlight without protective goggles. While the common man suffered under the brutal rays, the elite of Delhi found solace in air-conditioned establishments – shops, offices, and vehicles alike.

Dhurandhar Naik, the sole occupant of the solar energy-operated blue indigenous 'Mrugangi' car, steered it swiftly towards the airport. Following protocol, he drove himself, adhering to the well-established rule that on a highly classified mission, every defense officer should be behind the wheel. Even the most loyal driver was not to be relied upon. Only those deemed necessary were briefed, ensuring absolute secrecy. This principle, dating back to the times of Kautilya, was ingrained in every officer during their training.

Today, Naik awaited the arrival of a profoundly significant individual at the airport – Subhash, returning home via Beijing, Korea, and Myanmar after successfully completing 'Operation Black Diamond.' The chosen route, though circuitous, was a precautionary measure against potential pursuers from China. Naik, like everyone else, was kept in the dark about the specifics, adhering strictly to the 'need to know' principle. His duty was to pick up Subhash and escort him to the Ashwini Kumar Hospital, under the complete jurisdiction of the Defense Ministry, with further details known only to Naik.

Earlier that morning, Naik received a classified message from his superior, Mr. Parera, hinting at a possible breach in security regarding 'Operation Black Diamond.' Allegations suggested a leak from within the Ministry itself, jeopardizing Subhash's safety. The message also mentioned that information regarding Subhash's involvement in Operation Black Diamond had been leaked to the enemy camp. Had Subhash been abducted by the enemy or by the string operators, China would have been alerted. Indian spy had skillfully entered the fortress of China and set a trap. The secret mission would have failed, and the enemy would have retaliated. China would have gone to the U N O and made allegations against India, claiming that India had encroached upon their sovereignty.

Naik broke into a sweat at the implications – Subhash's abduction by the enemy would provoke an international crisis. Given recent tensions between India and China, any misstep could lead to dire consequences.

Had Subhash been abducted by the enemy or by the sting operators, China would have been alerted. Indian spy had skillfully entered the fortress of China and set a trap. The secret mission would have failed, and the enemy would have retaliated.

Recently, the Indian Military had achieved self-reliance, effectively thwarting the provocative actions and border skirmishes initiated by the Chinese military. These developments had left China fuming and searching for a pretext to condemn India on the international stage. India would have found itself in a precarious position with no solid arguments for defense, potentially escalating into a significant international crisis.

As Naik scanned the rear view mirror for signs of pursuit, he couldn't shake off the feeling of unease. Despite receiving clearance to use the secret military tunnel expressway, he remained vigilant, wary of any lurking threats. The security measures were impeccable. Mr. Naik couldn't enter the airport without going thorough check-up formalities.

Upon arriving at the airport, Naik carefully scanned the surroundings before spotting Subhash in the crowd. Subhash seemed to have shed a few pounds but appeared remarkably alert, his movements as nimble as ever. Carrying a backpack and a large suitcase, he managed his luggage effortlessly, his pace brisk and his eyes keenly observant.

There was no need for him to wait for security clearance; Mr. Naik had already arranged everything. Within thirty minutes, they were en route to Ashwini Kumar Hospital.

"Heartiest congratulations! Your courage and vigilance make operations like 'Black Diamond' possible. We are indebted to you," Naik commended, his eyes darting between the road and the rear view mirror.

Subhash, accustomed to such praise, couldn't conceal his satisfaction at the acknowledgment, his expression betraying a sense of pride.

"Thank you. It was an honor to be entrusted with this mission. The experience was exhilarating, akin to facing a lion in its den," Subhash replied, his tone reflecting a mix of humility and satisfaction.

"Moving forward, we must bury all knowledge of 'Operation Black Diamond.' Understood?" Naik inquired.

"What is 'Operation Black Diamond'? I've never heard of it," Subhash responded, his expression deadpan.

Naik's confusion quickly turned to amusement as he recognized the mischievous glint in Subhash's eyes. Together, they shared a moment of laughter.

"We're heading to a military hospital. You'll need to undergo a thorough examination to ensure your physical and mental well-being after the mission's strain. It's our new policy to ensure that our secret agents are kept under ideal conditions after every risky assignment. Mr. Parera has received a tip from secret yet reliable sources regarding this matter. Rest assured, you'll receive the best care," Naik explained as they approached the hospital gates, slowing down the car.

Naik couldn't tell if Subhash was convinced by this explanation. Even if Subhash was surprised by Naik's statement, it didn't show on his face.

At the gate of the hospital, they approached a booth designated for security checks. The armed guard instructed them to stop there for surveillance. He carefully inspected the credentials of both Mr. Naik and Subhash. After a brief conversation with Dr. Sehgal over the phone, the guard signaled for them to proceed, indicating they had received clearance from the doctor.

As a matter of fact, Mr. Naik had already communicated with Dr. Sehgal and the hospital administration regarding their arrival. He had informed Dr. Sehgal that he would be arriving with a patient. Despite this, he was not annoyed but rather pleased with the thorough security setup of the hospital.

Dr. Sehgal was waiting in his soundproof cabin. The moment Subhash was handed over to the hospital, half of Mr. Naik's responsibility would have been fulfilled. Once Subhash was treated by Dr. Sehgal and discharged from the hospital, Mr. Naik would have heaved a sigh of relief.

Dr. Sehgal received them cordially. Major Khatri had once said that half the ailment vanishes when a patient talks to him. His tall and stout build, along with his fair, handsome face, had a deep impact on the patient. Mr. Naik was reminded of these words every time he saw the doctor.

"I am entrusting you with my best man. I hope you will revitalize him," Mr. Naik said earnestly.

"Yes, I am aware of it. You may rest assured. After the treatment, he will rejuvenate," Dr. Sehgal replied confidently.

At that moment, a hospital ward boy came to fetch Subhash. Mr. Naik waved a hand at Subhash and looked expectantly at Dr. Sehgal.

"Our conversation is strictly confidential, and it should not reach another person. Subhash has just returned from a very risky mission, 'Operation Black Diamond'. Only two persons are aware of this operation. We do not want Subhash to remember a single word about this mission and his participation therein. This is extremely important. I have been informed by my superior that you would be able to accomplish it," Mr. Naik emphasized.

"I was already intimated about this job when you called me in the morning. We have been researching on the human brain. We concentrated on a particular part of the brain called the hippocampus and its functioning," Dr. Sehgal replied assuredly.

Dr. Sehgal brought up an image of the human brain on the screen of his laptop and said, "I will explain to you what we did. That will make you comprehend what we propose to do."

"I would love that. But please, tell me what is absolutely necessary and what a layman like me would be able to grasp," replied Mr. Naik, eager to understand.

"You must be aware that in western countries, scientists have taken a lot of interest in the human brain, and they have been working on it. Of course, in ancient times, even Indian scholars worked on the human brain, but they perceived it as the mind and intellect. They presumed there to be layers of the human brain and its understanding power," explained Dr. Sehgal.

"In a way, it is true, but we have never delved into the structure of the brain and its components. We have not explored the physical parts of the brain. There is no literature on that. But that is not what I want to discuss with you. The human brain is divided into the left and right parts. Below the left and right cerebral cortex, there is an organ called the hippocampus," Dr. Sehgal explained.

"For many years, scientists presumed that cells in the cortex store memories. However, in the absence of concrete evidence, this theory remained unproven. In 2014, it was demonstrated that every cell in the cortex stores a specific memory. Now, let me simplify it for you," Dr. Sehgal continued.

"Just as we store our information on a single topic in a single file for our benefit, so does the brain. Just as we can easily retrieve this info whenever necessary, the brain works in the same manner. Once this was proved, scientists started thinking in a different direction," Dr. Sehgal explained.

"Oh! I got it. Once you know the source cell of a particular memory, it became possible to manipulate or erase that memory," Mr. Naik finished Dr. Sehgal's sentence, now understanding the implications of the research.

"Other sciences had also advanced in the meantime. Scientists began exploring electronic methods to identify this storage system, aiming to segregate memories and determine the source cell of each one. As you're aware, there was significant progress across various fields in India during the third decade of this century. Numerous research institutes emerged, diligently working in their respective domains." Dr Sehgal stared at Mr Naik and Naik nodded in affirmation.

"They were interconnected through information technology, facilitating the completion of many interdisciplinary projects. Two years ago, one of our teams developed a machine capable of calculating microscopic vibrations from each cell. Consequently, the prospects of identifying cells based on the memories they stored appeared promising for the future. Once you know the source cell of a particular memory, it becomes possible to precisely target and manipulate individual memories, potentially leading to significant advancements in various fields, including medicine, psychology, and artificial intelligence."

"Oh my God!" exclaimed Mr Naik.

"To identify the cell, all you have to do is stimulate that particular cell. If you make the person think about that event, you can stimulate the cell by its vibrations. If one is successful in removing that particular cell from his brain, the memory would be wiped off permanently."

"Fantastic! I can't believe it."

"But there is one hitch. We will have to segregate those memories which we wish to remove from the rest, and for that we have to kindle those specific memories by injecting some stimulants. For a couple of years, we were attempting to achieve this, but without success. It presented a significant challenge—how to stimulate a specific memory? At last, we succeeded in our mission. We have successfully tested our procedure on a reasonably large sample."

"I got your point but how long would it take?" asked Mr Naik.

"I understand your concern, but it's difficult to provide an exact time frame," replied Dr. Sehgal. "It depends on various factors, including the complexity of the memories and the individual's response to the treatment. However, we will do our best to expedite the process while ensuring its effectiveness. There's no issue regarding the time required. Stimulants are of two types. We can inject one stimulant in the human body. This stimulant works as a catalyst to speed up the process of thought. The issue of reaching the identified memory is a tricky one. We can induce the person to think about it by talking about the concerned subject. He will never talk to us if we ask him about the mission. He will either prefer to keep mum or mislead us. He would deliberately divert his mind to other subjects. Here I will need your assistance. However, if we directly ask him about the mission, he may choose to remain silent or divert his mind deliberately. This is where I'll need your assistance."

Mr. Naik was in a fix. He started pondering over the situation, trying to devise a plan.

"I am ready to help you. What do you want me to do?"

"You may either tell what this mission was about or.."

"That is out of question" Mr Naik replied before Dr Sehgal could complete his sentence.

"Then you yourself may ask him some questions about it. But at least I will have to be present while you talk to him." Dr Sehgal suggested.

After contemplating on this issue for a few minutes, Mr. Naik found a way out.

"Alright, I understand. I'll ask him a few leading questions that won't reveal anything. Let's proceed. Just let me know when," he replied.

"We will have to hypnotize him," Dr. Sehgal suggested.

Mr. Naik had no reason to protest. They decided to start the procedure the next morning.

Mr. Naik felt considerably more at ease now that the procedure date was scheduled. So much so that he inadvertently began whistling his favorite Hindi song. If this experiment proved successful, he would be completely relieved. Moreover, his promotion was imminent. If he successfully concluded this task, his promotion was practically assured.

At that moment, he had no doubts about the potential side effects of the treatment. However, later on, his mind began to ponder the potential implications of the procedure. It was relatively straightforward to ascertain whether Subhash had indeed lost all memories related to Operation Black Diamond. However, what would he recall about his activities during that period? How would he explain his absence from India to others?

At night, Mr. Naik struggled to sleep due to these doubts. Could the removed memories be replaced by other false ones? He drifted off while contemplating this possibility. When he woke up at six in the morning, the first thing that crossed his mind was the necessity of discussing this issue with Dr. Sehgal. Hastily completing his morning routine, he made his way to the hospital.

Dr. Sehgal was prepared, but Mr. Naik wanted to address his doubts first. Dr. Sehgal assured Mr. Naik that the procedure would not have any damaging effects on the patient. Furthermore, he explained that the procedure would only erase memories related to the mission, not the entire one-month period. Dr. Sehgal dismissed Mr. Naik's suggestion of implanting false memories in place of the removed ones. Subhash would retain memories of being in China and visiting other sites, but he would have no recollection of Operation Black Diamond. It was indeed a tricky situation.

"Doctor, I need to share a crucial point with you. If Subhash isn't made to forget about his other activities during that period, we won't achieve the desired effect. Even if he forgets the reason for his trip to China, he'll still recall being there. While he's under hypnosis, I could suggest to him that he went to

China as a tourist. Can't we implant that idea in his mind?" Mr. Naik inquired.

Dr. Sehgal pondered over it for a few moments before consenting.

"You must be certain about what you want him to believe. Suggestions made to a person under hypnosis can be difficult to undo," he cautioned.

Dr. Sehgal led Mr. Naik into the procedure room, which bore little resemblance to a typical hospital room. Instead, it resembled a state-of-the-art laboratory, impressing Mr. Naik with its advanced technology. The room was separated from the observation area by a glass wall, providing a clear view of the interior. Inside, a young technician wearing something resembling a headphone was busy adjusting wires on various apparatuses.

Numerous electronic devices, along with tangled wires, filled the glass cupboards lining the opposite wall of the procedure room. On the table, a few electronic gadgets awaited use. As Dr. Sehgal and Mr. Naik stood alone in the room, Mr. Naik couldn't shake the feeling of unease caused by the technician's presence in the adjacent room. He suspected that the technician might inadvertently overhear their conversation with Subhash.

Dr. Sehgal assured Mr. Naik that the technician's presence in the adjacent room was essential for the procedure. To alleviate Mr. Naik's concerns, Dr. Sehgal explained that the room was completely soundproof, ensuring that the technician wouldn't be able to overhear their conversation. This reassurance put Mr. Naik at ease, allowing him to focus on the task at hand.

Dr. Sehgal deftly managed the wires connected to the intricate machines as he conversed with Mr. Naik. Subhash was wheeled into the room in a wheelchair, his head covered with a thin cap-like device. With gentle care, they positioned him on the bed beneath the bright lamp. Dr. Sehgal administered a medicine into Subhash's vein, initiating the procedure.

"Every cell in your body and your mind will receive vitality and energy now that this medicine is injected," Dr. Sehgal reassured Subhash in a soothing tone, his voice resonating deeply. Continuing to speak softly, he swiftly induced Subhash into a hypnotic state. With a nod to Mr. Naik, Dr. Sehgal signaled that Subhash was ready.

"Subhash, can you hear me? Do you understand what I am saying?" Dr. Sehgal inquired, his voice gentle yet firm.

Subhash responded with a single nod.

"Now, you are going to follow Mr. Dhurandhar Naik's instructions. Do you understand?" Dr. Sehgal clarified, then deftly approached the operation table, connecting numerous thin wires to Subhash's helmet with remarkable skill.

Once more, Subhash nodded in acknowledgment of Dr. Sehgal's query.

Dr. Sehgal signaled to Mr. Naik to initiate the conversation.

Mr. Naik cleared his throat and began, "Subhash, it was my decision to send you for Operation Black Diamond. And as events unfolded, my decision was proven to be wise. That's why I am proud of you."

Dr. Sehgal keenly observed the screen of a machine, resembling a keyboard and mouse, clicking away. He signaled to Mr. Naik to continue speaking.

"I had summoned you to Delhi and briefed you on the proposed Operation Black Diamond. Can you recall your initial reaction to the news?"

"Of course, I remember. Initially, I perceived the plan as frail. It seemed highly risky and improbable, with a couple of apparent loopholes."

"When did you start believing in its potential for success?"

"Shall I tell you the truth? I was never convinced. No matter how meticulously planned, there are always uncertainties. You admitted it yourself."

"For two days, we meticulously crafted the plan. Only the two of us knew the details."

"We agreed that once the mission commenced, I shouldn't contact you under any circumstance."

"We spent two days planning," Mr. Naik reiterated.

Mr. Naik continued to pose seemingly irrelevant and superficial questions to Subhash, struggling to maintain his engagement without divulging any sensitive information.

As the 'bip, bip' sound emitted from the machine, indicating the successful identification of the targeted cells, the technician on the other side of the glass wall gave a thumbs-up sign, signaling their achievement.

Noticing this, Dr. Sehgal conveyed the same message to Mr. Naik through a raised hand gesture, wordlessly confirming their progress.

Mr. Naik felt a wave of relief wash over him. He had doubted his ability to sustain a seemingly innocuous conversation on the topic without inadvertently revealing sensitive information. However, abruptly halting the dialogue would have been unwise. Therefore, he pressed on.

"We refrained from any contact during the operation. Remarkably, you completed the mission in just two days. Your performance was so exceptional that the Department rewarded you with a trip to the eastern countries. It was funded from the President's special budget, which unfortunately meant you couldn't bring your family along. Do you remember that trip?"

For a few seconds, Subhash didn't respond, but then nodded in affirmation. Dr. Sehgal signaled for Mr. Naik to remain silent. Mr. Naik wiped the perspiration from his forehead, let out a sigh of relief, and sank into his chair.

Dr. Sehgal murmured softly, "You are fast asleep now. We won't disturb you for a few minutes. Your body feels as light as a feather. You need complete rest. You are fast asleep."

Dr. Sehgal carefully removed the helmet from Subhash's head and positioned a minuscule drill on a pr-identified point on his skull. With precision, he extracted a cell onto a slide using a laser beam and delicately transferred it into a small, sterilized, germ-free test tube. Placing the test tube into a specially manufactured fridge designed for this purpose, he ensured the cell remained preserved.

Naik wrote a message on a piece of paper: 'You can preserve and store it in your archive.' Dr. Sehgal nodded in acknowledgment. After the procedure, it was relatively easy to bring Subhash out of hypnosis and escort him back to his room. The process didn't take much time. The following day, with utmost security measures in place, the concerned cell was transported to the secret archives of the Defense Department. Naik breathed a sigh of relief, knowing that the vital piece of information was now safely secured.

Mr. Naik visited Subhash in the hospital room after two days. During their conversation, he carefully avoided any mention of the secret mission on which Subhash was sent. However, Naik subtly introduced terms like "Black Pearl" and "Black Diamond" into their discussion, ensuring that Subhash did not recall their significance in relation to the covert operation.

There was not even the slightest change of expression on Subhash's face as he recounted his recent visit to eastern countries to Mr. Naik. He made sure to mention that it was a gift from the Department, expressing a subtle sense of pride in his voice. Dr. Sehgal had already confirmed the efficacy of the procedure by conversing with Subhash while he was hypnotized again.

Mr. Naik profusely thanked Dr. Sehgal for his invaluable assistance. Dr. Sehgal, in turn, warned Mr. Naik about the importance of keeping the experiment strictly confidential. If news about this groundbreaking procedure were to leak out, other nations would stop at nothing to acquire the knowledge. Both were acutely aware of this reality.

The dismissal of three ministers in China and the ensuing havoc in the nation's industrial world in recent days were clear indications of the success of Operation Black Diamond. Both Mr. Parera and Mr. Naik were fully aware of this fact. Now, Mr. Naik was certain that his promotion would be imminent.

After a week, Mr. Naik received an urgent email on his personal computer from Mr. Malhotra. Subhash had reached home safely, but he absconded the next day. Mr. Malhotra and his team had left no stone unturned but couldn't find a single clue. Nobody knew where he went or with whom. He had not contacted anybody since his disappearance.

"It smelt of enemy intervention," Mr. Naik said, his voice tinged with concern, as he went to see Dr. Sehgal. Despite Dr. Sehgal's reassurances that the procedure was foolproof and Subhash wouldn't be able to reveal anything about the mission, both Mr. Naik and Mr. Parera spent sleepless nights.

Subhash was discovered on the streets of Mumbai a week later. Late at night, unknown individuals had dropped him off in the bustling streets of the city. Upon his arrival, he promptly contacted Mr. Naik, who hastily made his way to Mumbai. Mr. Naik met with Subhash and conducted a thorough interrogation. Subhash recounted his ordeal, describing how the kidnappers appeared to be Chinese and had kept him confined in a dark, cell-like room.

They had subjected him to torture, relentlessly inquiring about Operation Black Diamond. Their questions echoed in Subhash's mind: "Who had entrusted you with the responsibility of Operation Black Diamond? What was the motive behind your recent visit to China?" Subhash was utterly perplexed because he was completely unaware of the mission Operation Black Diamond. All he could tell them was that he had visited China as a tourist. He remained bewildered as to why the Chinese Intelligence Department took such a keen interest in his visit.

He was honest with Mr. Naik, expressing his confusion over the interrogation. How could he have divulged information about things he had no knowledge of? Subhash endured beatings and torture until he lost consciousness and was callously discarded on the streets. Upon his discovery, Mr. Malhotra and the high command at the Defense Ministry were promptly notified. This incident couldn't be dismissed lightly.

Dr. Sehgal, Mr. Naik, and Mr. Parera received summons to the President's office for the following day. Aware of the gravity of the situation, Mr. Parera and Mr. Naik braced themselves for intense interrogation and a barrage of questions. No one wished to bear the brunt of failure. Their sole defense lay in the flawless medical treatment administered to

Subhash, which thwarted the kidnappers' attempts to extract information from him.

As the three entered the President's office, they were greeted by the presence of the Defense Minister, signaling a far more significant development than they had expected.

The Defense Minister extended his hand to each of them and began, "I congratulate you three on your success. Both Operation Black Diamond and Dr. Sehgal's experiment have proven successful. This is a significant leap forward, Doctor."

Mr. Parera and Mr. Naik were left speechless, stunned by the unexpected turn of events. The Minister continued, "I must confess and apologize for one thing. We checked the effectiveness of your experiment in our own way but kept you in the dark about it. Subhash was kidnapped by none other than our own intelligence bureau."

The revelation left them stunned, processing the implications of the Minister's words.

"But according to Subhash's statement, the kidnappers were Chinese," Mr. Parera expressed his doubt.

"They were our own people from Nagaland, specially trained for this mission. We chose them because of the similarity between their facial features and those of the Chinese," the Minister clarified. "We wanted to be one hundred per cent sure about the effectiveness of Dr. Sehgal's experiment. It was essential not to confide in you. To our knowledge, the news about

Subhash's mission had not leaked, but we could not rule out that possibility," the Minister explained.

Mr. Naik's face flushed with agitation. He asked, "At the risk of Subhash's life? He is one of our best agents."

This time, it was the President who replied in a serious and convincing tone.

"We had taken due precautions not to harm Subhash in any way. We have to engage in such strategies even with our own people if we are to maintain our highest ranking in the international community. We have struggled immensely to attain this position."

....

Generation Gap

Uma had been glued to her computer screen for hours on end, her eyes growing weary with fatigue. Craving a break, she longed for a comforting cup of steaming ginger tea. Yet, in this unfamiliar land, such simple pleasures seemed out of reach. Settling for a glass of coffee from the vending machine, she reluctantly abandoned her hopes of tea.

Just as she prepared to vacate her desk, a notification signaled the arrival of a new email. Intrigued, Uma couldn't resist checking her inbox, where she found a message from Sarita.

"The mail read, 'Accommodation available. 2 vacancies. Jagan's roommate moving out. Are you interested? Waiting for your reply.' It seemed like a straightforward offer, but Uma found herself perplexed. She wasn't ready to respond immediately. Unsure of whether to accept or decline, she opted for a neutral response: 'Coming to see you.' With a sigh, she powered down her computer, eager to alleviate the strain in her tired muscles. Grabbing her purse, she made her way to Sarita's cabin on the eighth floor."

Each time such situations arose, Uma found herself reflecting on the rapidly evolving environment around her. Everything seemed to be in a state of constant flux. Values were shifting at an alarming pace, a stark contrast to what she remembered from her own upbringing.

The phrase "when we were young" echoed in her mind, causing her to pause in disbelief. What did she mean by "our times"? She certainly didn't consider herself old. At twenty-eight, she was still in the prime of her life. Sarita, her colleague and friend, was only three years her junior. So why did Uma often feel like she was light-years ahead in experience? Why did she sense a growing disconnect from the mainstream?

It wasn't just Sarita; Uma felt this sense of detachment around all the new recruits in the company. Despite being in her twenties, she couldn't shake off the feeling of being out of sync with the younger generation.

"Why do I feel such a stark generation gap when I'm around them?" Uma mused, pondering the source of her disconnection. "Is it simply because I hold a senior position within the company? Or is it that while the world around me has been evolving rapidly, I've remained stagnant in comparison? Could it be that the bitter experiences of the past few years have aged me prematurely, and I've been unaware of the transformation taking place within me?" She couldn't help but question her own perception of herself and her place in the world, grappling with the unsettling realization that perhaps she had been oblivious to the changes occurring within her until now.

Glancing over at Sarita's cabin, Uma couldn't help but notice Sarita's outfit for the day: light green trousers paired with a black short top. Uma observed that the ensemble made Sarita appear somewhat chubby, a detail she couldn't overlook. Despite Sarita's open-mindedness and talkative nature, Uma couldn't help but notice how she subtly tried to conceal the curves of her chest by leaning slightly forward. It was a gesture that betrayed a hint of self-consciousness, even when dressed in Western attire, a departure from the easy confidence typically seen in American young women. Despite this, Sarita seemed visibly excited at the prospect of securing new accommodation. 'The project was slated to last for six months,' Uma reflected, drawing from her past experiences. 'But judging from the last project, it wouldn't be surprising if it extended for a couple more months.'

"Can't you see how beneficial this arrangement would be for us?" Uma reasoned, emphasizing the advantages to her companion. "We won't have to worry about the lease, and raising the deposit money would be next to impossible for us. Plus, none of us own a car, but these boys do. Imagine navigating these crowded roads with right-hand drive and unfamiliar traffic rules. If we had a car, who would even want to drive? We'd likely be stuck taking the metro, which would mean early mornings and added hassle. With this setup, we'll be relieved of all those troubles."

"I do understand these advantages. But..." Uma began, her voice trailing off as she hesitated to express her full thoughts.

"We would feel much safer in this unknown country with these boys around us," Sarita interjected, her excitement evident. "We're still not acclimatized to the weather conditions and social environment here. Plus, it'll be so much easier to handle weekly grocery shopping and other errands with their help. Opportunities like this don't come often."

Lost in her own thoughts, Sarita didn't immediately notice Uma's hesitance. But as the moments passed, she couldn't ignore it any longer. Turning to Uma, she asked, "What's your problem, yaar? Aren't you relieved? We've been paying a fortune for those dingy hotel rooms... Wait, have you already made separate arrangements for your stay?"

"Don't be silly. I wouldn't ditch you," Uma reassured Sarita, but her curiosity lingered. "But tell me, how did all of this happen so quickly? Did Jagan suggest that we move in? How did he even know we were looking for accommodation?"

"Not just him, but everyone in our office knows we're in need of a place to stay," Sarita explained. "Yesterday night, he mentioned that he'd have to find new roommates. I saw it as an opportunity and seized it. What harm is there in that?"

Uma felt a wave of relief knowing that Jagan hadn't initiated the plan. Yet, she couldn't help but wonder about the intentions behind such proposals when they come from men. How can we be certain that their motives are pure and honorable?

But then from boys' perspective, there's always a risk of misinterpretation, especially if the proposal had come from a woman. Boys might easily misconstrue the intentions, leading to misunderstandings. It's a delicate balance to navigate, Uma realized, fraught with potential complications.

"Did you bring up the topic?" Uma inquired.

"Of course, I did. It seemed prudent to stake our claim before anyone else did," Sarita replied confidently.

"That's true... What was his response?" Uma pressed further.

"He was okay with it," Sarita answered. "And he mentioned that he's looking forward to enjoying some delicious meals now that there are ladies in the house. I had to remind him not to get his hopes up," Sarita added with a mischievous smile, continuing, "It's a 2 BHK flat. We'll share one room, while Jagan and Kartik will share the other. We'll have to use the kitchen together, and expenses will be split equally. The lease is in Jagan's name, and he's offered to take us there in his car."

"Do you really know him well? How long have you known him?" Uma questioned, her tone tinged with doubt.

"What does it matter? We're just sharing a flat. We don't know anyone here," Sarita responded dismissively. "Local customs and ideas can be different, and there's risk no matter where we decide to stay. At least with Jagan, he's our colleague. We've known him for a while. We worked in the same branch back home for one and a half years. He's always been well-behaved."

"What about the other guy, Kartik? Is he from our office too?" Uma pressed on.

"Yes, he is, but unlike us, he's from T C S. He's not as outgoing and friendly as Jagan, but he's a decent and reserved guy," Sarita answered confidently.

Uma couldn't help but marvel at Sarita's certainty in labeling Kartik as sober and decent. Was it really that easy to assess someone's character? She reflected on her own experiences, remembering how she had once thought Vishvesh, a software engineer from Mumbai branch of her office, was also decent and sober. But ultimately, she had learned the hard way that appearances could be deceiving.

Her maternal uncle from Delhi had enthusiastically suggested Vishvesh's name to her parents for a marriage proposal. He spoke highly of Vishvesh, his excitement palpable with every mention of the young man. Vishvesh, an engineer working in a software company and currently based in Chennai, seemed like an ideal match. Daddy was particularly pleased with the proposal, noting Vishvesh's membership in their own caste and his impressive academic and professional achievements. Everything seemed to align perfectly – from their ages and physical appearance to the compatibility of their horoscopes. Mummy couldn't help but exhale a sigh of relief at the prospect of such a promising match.

Grandma's relief was palpable as she joyfully blessed Uma upon hearing about the proposal. Even if Vishvesh hadn't been particularly handsome, Uma would have accepted the proposal without hesitation, given the unanimous approval of the elders. However, Uma found herself attracted to Vishvesh's looks as well. His handsome face, wheatish complexion, and warm smile all contributed to his appeal in her eyes.

There was seemingly nothing to turn down about Vishvesh. His parents appeared elite and educated, further adding to the allure of the proposal. Uma's parents were overjoyed, leaving no room for complaint from Vishvesh's family. They accommodated all their requests, including the choice of venue and the style of celebration. Yet, despite their best intentions, the outcome was far from what anyone had anticipated. The money invested in the wedding seemed to have gone to waste, and Uma found herself labeled as a divorcee—a painful reminder of the past that she tried to push away. At that very moment interrupted Sarita unaware of the turbulent chapter in Uma's life.

"Uma, what are you so engrossed in?" Sarita's question snapped Uma back to the present.

"Would your parents approve of you sharing quarters with boys?" Uma inquired cautiously.

"To be honest, I'm not going to seek their approval," Sarita replied boldly. "I'll simply inform them that I'm sharing a room with you. That should suffice, shouldn't it? In a way that is the truth. If they happen to find out the truth later on, I'll deal with the problem when it arises."

Uma couldn't help but admire Sarita's audacity and courage. Perhaps, she mused, North Indian girls are indeed more outgoing and daring than their South Indian counterparts.

'Whether it was my mistake or not, the fact remains that I am labeled as a divorcee,' Uma lamented. 'If I were to go ahead with something like this, it could tarnish my reputation. It's well-known that divorcees are often taken for granted and advantage of... Men always think along these lines.' That made Uma declare hesitantly,

"I wouldn't be able to decide immediately. I need some time to think about it,"

"Come on, yaar. Be a sport. No one pays that much attention to these traditional norms anymore," Sarita urged, unaware of Uma's inner turmoil. "Let me tell you something. My experience of sharing rooms with girls in Bangalore wasn't very pleasant. They tend to be narrow-minded, arguing over trivial matters, and constantly comparing themselves to one another. It's exhausting to deal with such pettiness. Boys, on the other hand, are more straightforward and easier to get along with." Sarita expressed her opinion without realizing that she herself belonged to the group she was criticizing. However, Uma couldn't help but acknowledge that her own experiences with girls weren't much different from Sarita's.

"Okay, I won't let you down. Since you've already made up your mind, I'll accompany you to Jagan's place," Uma declared in her usual cautious manner.

"Not bad! Now give me a smile. Don't worry about all the problems faced by mankind," teased Sarita, playfully punching Uma's stomach and tossing her head back to adjust the strands of hair falling on her forehead before bursting into laughter.

This innocent gesture seemed to transfer the lightheartedness from Sarita to Uma. Unconsciously, it brought a smile to Uma's face.

"So we're meeting in the evening, right?" Uma confirmed.

....

"We're waiting at the gate. Are you on your way?" Sarita's voice came through the phone.

Uma glanced at her wristwatch. She hadn't finished today's work, but it wasn't urgent enough to keep her friends waiting. "I'll be there in five minutes," she replied before shutting down her computer. Quickly clearing her desk and stashing the keys to her locker in her purse, Uma made a brief stop at the restroom to freshen up before heading downstairs.

Sarita, Jagan, and Kartik were waiting for her at the main gate. Uma apologized for the delay, and the four of them climbed into Jagan's car. The apartment was about half an hour's drive from the office. The community was pleasant, with well-kept houses and neatly maintained patches of flower beds and lawns. Artificial rocks added to the landscape, while tall green trees provided a soothing backdrop. In the center of the community, there was a swimming pool where a few Indians were lingering. Nearby, a few shops were visible at a short distance.

The apartment had a sturdy latch on the door, providing a sense of security. Despite being a two-story building, there was a lift available for convenience. As Uma and Sarita entered, they found the flat to be well-maintained by the pair. Despite the visit being unplanned, the space was remarkably clean and tidy. Both the drawing room and kitchen were immaculate, equipped with modern amenities such as a cooking range, microwave oven, TV set, and DVD player.

The flat surpassed their expectations, especially considering the ones they had audited in the last couple of days. The room they were to share was spacious, with a large closet for storage. Although there were no beds, thick mattresses were provided, ensuring a comfortable rest. There was ample room to move around, and they could enjoy views of the blue sky and lush greenery from the window.

"Let's clear a few things at the outset," Jagan stated firmly. "We've established some rules for our home, and they apply to all residents of this flat. We distribute daily duties among ourselves, including cleaning, shopping, and cooking. We even take turns cleaning the restrooms. From now on, you'll be responsible for cleaning your own bathroom. When rules are clearly outlined, it's better for everyone involved. We prefer to maintain a harmonious atmosphere in the house and avoid unnecessary arguments that can pollute the environment." Jagan's words were blunt but direct, leaving no room for misunderstanding.

"Ayla! It's okay with all other duties but sharing cooking is too much. We never did that even in Banglore. I am a strict vegetarian. Hence I keep my separate utensils." said Sarita. She glanced at Uma for support.

"Absolutely! I understand your concerns, Sarita," Uma chimed in, offering her support. "We're used to cooking separately as well. Everyone has their own dietary preferences and budget constraints."

"Regardless of individual preferences, we have our rules," Jagan interjected firmly. "We cook fish or chicken once a week and consume eggs daily. Our former roommate, Shailesh, was a strict vegetarian, but he managed just fine. On days when we prepare non-vegetarian dishes, we also make sure to include a vegetarian option. There's no need to keep track of who consumes what. All expenses incurred are divided equally among us."

Sarita and Uma exchanged glances, silently acknowledging the need to adapt to the established norms of the household.

"We divide the rent and grocery expenses equally," Jagan explained further. "That comes to around $250 for rent per person and approximately $250 for other expenses, including travel and eating out on weekends. Everyone is expected to cover their own gas expenses according to their usage. Since you don't own a car, the carpool option is available for you. However, you'll need to share the expenses if we provide transportation to and from the office."

Initially, Uma and Sarita had perceived Jagan as friendly and cordial, but it was becoming evident that he was outspoken and direct, particularly when it came to financial matters. Perhaps his extended stay in the USA had made him more forthright compared to other Desies. However, Uma couldn't help but think that it's better to be straightforward than to foster misunderstandings and arguments. Despite this, it was clear that Kartik was growing uneasy with Jagan's somewhat arrogant demeanor.

Kartik interjected, likely sensing the tension in the room and hoping to steer the conversation towards a more positive direction.

"One thing I must tell you," he began, "we've never had serious arguments with any of our roommates, and there hasn't been a single occasion for which to repent."

His words were a gentle reminder that despite any differences or challenges they might face, their past experiences had been relatively conflict-free and without regrets. It was a subtle attempt to diffuse any lingering discomfort and foster a sense of camaraderie among them.

As Uma reflected on her past experiences with roommates in Bangalore, she couldn't help but recall the challenges she had faced. Living with Kanan and Sumitra had been far from ideal.

Kanan's habits were particularly bothersome. Her untidy and dirty living conditions made Uma cringe. She often neglected her duties, especially when it came to cleaning the dishes, and her bed was perpetually covered in heaps of used clothes. The sight of her fallen hair scattered throughout the room made Uma feel nauseated, prompting her to delay entering their flat whenever possible.

On the other hand, Sumitra presented a different set of issues. While she was stingy with sharing her own food, she had no qualms about helping herself to Uma's belongings. Despite never contributing to the household groceries, she didn't hesitate to consume Uma's expensive perfume or even snacks sent by Uma's mother, shamelessly claiming to love them.

Uma couldn't deny that her past experiences with roommates had been far from harmonious, unlike the amicable living situation Jagan and Sarita described.

Uma vividly remembered the day when the tension with her former roommates, Kanan and Sumitra, reached its breaking point. Kanan's accusation that Uma thought herself superior and was a snob for engaging in reading sparked a fiery confrontation. Sumitra had also chimed in, escalating the situation into a heated argument. Reflecting on it now, Uma realized that the lack of open communication and unresolved tensions had contributed to the explosive incident.

Her reminiscences were interrupted by Jagan's voice, bringing her back to the present moment.

"All these details can be sorted out in due course," Jagan stated calmly. "But I want you to understand how we live and what our expectations are. Take some time to think about it and let us know your decision within two days. I won't be offended if you choose not to move in. If your answer is negative, I'll start looking for a new roommate."

Jagan's words were considerate and gave Uma the space to make a decision without pressure. It was a stark contrast to the confrontational dynamics she had experienced in the past, reminding her that open communication and mutual respect were key to maintaining a harmonious living environment.

Uma couldn't help but ponder the stark differences between her generation and the one represented by Jagan and his peers. She admired Jagan's frankness and ability to express his thoughts without hesitation or pretense. There was a refreshing lack of awkwardness and false chivalry in his demeanor.

Yet, Uma found herself hesitating at the notion of being part of this new generation. Could she adapt to their way of communication and interaction? Was it possible for her to shed the constraints of her own upbringing and embrace this more open approach?

The word "generation" made Uma flinch. Was there truly a significant generation gap between individuals with only a 2 or 3-year age difference? Uma wasn't convinced. She believed that it was more about the rapid evolution of times rather than a rigid divide between generations. Despite her admiration for Jagan's candor, Uma acknowledged her struggle to keep pace with the rapidly changing world around her.

It was Kartik once again who attempted to lighten the mood, bringing a tray with cups of tea and snacks. "The Indian store is quite nearby, so..." he declared, offering the refreshments.

The gesture helped ease the tension, and soon they found themselves engaged in conversation on various topics without constraint. As they offered to drop Uma and Sarita back to their quarters, Jagan demonstrated his consideration by suggesting a stop at Taco Bell along the way. "It's on the house" he declared with a hint of mirth in his otherwise neutral eyes.

This act of thoughtfulness made Uma reconsider her initial impression of Jagan's perceived curtness. She found herself appreciating his frankness, and his polite manners made his behavior more acceptable. It became evident that his intentions were not as narrow-minded or miserly as they may have seemed at first. However, Uma still struggled to fully appreciate his moneycentric approach.

As they made their way back, Sarita's unusually quiet demeanor caught Uma's attention. It seemed that her enthusiasm for moving in with Jagan had waned. Was she disheartened by the realization that Jagan might not bend to her wishes?

By the time Sarita retired to bed, she had resolved to proceed with the proposition. However, she grappled with the idea of common cooking and preparing non-vegetarian dishes in the same vessels. She suspected that Jagan wouldn't compromise on these matters. While discussing it with Uma, Sarita attempted to rationalize her decision, suggesting that eating out at restaurants serving both vegetarian and non-vegetarian cuisines made cooking non-vegetarian dishes at home less objectionable.

Uma could see that like her Sarita too was trying to convince herself the desirability of sharing quarters with Jagan and finding justifications for that decision. She too was trying to cross the mental barriers. But obviously Uma's barriers were far more serious than Sarita's. Her struggle was against the deep rooted values and need to take practical decision in the given situation.

"My mental hurdle is quite different from yours." said Uma, "My parents will never like me staying with unknown youths. And to be frank with you, even I do not approve of it."

"Come on yaar, You are talking like oldies, my mom and aunts. The girls that wish to flirt with boys need not stay with them. It can be achieved in many other ways. Mom can never understand this point. We know of many such places which are rented on hourly basis for this purpose even in India. This is rampant in bigger cities in almost every state." Sarita bluntly said.

It once again reminded Uma of her ex spouse Vishvesh.

As Uma reminisced about the incident that had exposed Vishvesh's betrayal, she found herself reliving the emotions she had tried so hard to bury in the past. Despite her lack of experience, she wasn't completely ignorant about the nature of sexual relationships between a man and a woman. However, on her wedding night, she couldn't shake off the nervousness that accompanied the thought of allowing an unknown man to touch her body.

That night had been exhausting, with endless hours of conventional wedding rituals, the heat of the holy fire, and the repetition of mantras. Laden with heavy ornaments and draped in an intricate brocade sari, Uma felt suffocated by the weight of tradition. Half of the guests were strangers to her, yet she was expected to engage with them, maintaining a perpetual smile on her sweaty face. Amidst the chaos, the only solace had been the romantic moments shared with Vishvesh and the teasing from her close friends. But little did she know then that those moments would soon be tainted by betrayal.

As Uma timidly stepped into the room, she was engulfed by a whirlwind of emotions—a mixture of anticipation for tender moments, shyness, and the fear of the unknown. All she longed for was a simple heart-to-heart conversation with her newfound life partner—nothing more. She yearned for Vishvesh to show tenderness in his touch and to speak warm words to her on that occasion. For Uma, marriage was a union of two hearts, and she believed there was no place for physical intimacy unless there was mutual love and understanding between partners.

Despite her expectations, Uma was pleasantly surprised when Vishvesh acted exactly as she had hoped. He seemed to comprehend Uma's apprehensions and respected her boundaries. In that moment, Uma felt a deep sense of gratitude towards Vishvesh for his considerate nature. He had refrained from insisting on physical intimacy, which made Uma feel understood and cherished. It was a moment that solidified her admiration for him and left her eagerly anticipating deeper intimacy in the days to come. In Vishvesh's actions, Uma found a source of pride and comfort, knowing that she had chosen a partner who valued her feelings and respected her boundaries.

The reason behind Vishvesh's peculiar behavior became apparent when Uma received a phone call from her cousin, Shrikant, just a week after the wedding. He requested Uma to meet him outside his office building after her work hours.

Anticipating Shrikant's usual jovial demeanor, Uma was taken aback by the seriousness in his tone. Despite her attempts to glean more information from him, Shrikant remained tight-lipped. Uma's worry for her parents prompted her to inquire about their health, but Shrikant's cryptic responses only heightened her concern. He emphasized that she shouldn't worry about "*them,*" a statement that set off alarm bells in Uma's mind.

Despite her persistent questioning, Shrikant refused to divulge any further details over the phone and insisted on meeting Uma in person.

Their meeting revealed that Vishvesh had been spotted at the infamous Hotel Paradise, known for its involvement in unlawful activities and clandestine rendezvous, especially for extramarital affairs. Shrikant's suspicions had proven to be true, shedding light on Vishvesh's secretive behavior.

Having lived a simple and virtuous life thus far, Uma was unwilling to tolerate adultery and deceit in her married life. For her, integrity and character were of the utmost importance. Despite her shock and heartache, Uma chose to voice her grievances while shedding tears in front of her in-laws, instead opting to keep the knowledge of Vishvesh's infidelity to herself.

In response, Vishvesh remained silent, offering no defense for his actions, while his parents chose not to intervene. Their silence spoke volumes, revealing that they were aware of Vishvesh's extramarital affair. Vishvesh showed no remorse or willingness to change his behavior.

Faced with the painful truth and Vishvesh's lack of remorse, Uma made a difficult decision. She called her parents and informed them of her intention to seek a divorce by mutual consent, effectively ending her marriage to Vishvesh. It was a heartbreaking but necessary step for Uma to preserve her integrity and seek a life free from deception and betrayal.

Uma's parents had lived a life deeply rooted in tradition, and the idea of divorce was something they would never have condoned. However, faced with the painful reality of Vishvesh's infidelity and Uma's unhappiness, they reluctantly gave their consent for a divorce by mutual agreement. Despite the success of the legal process, it was a deeply painful experience for Uma and her parents.

In the aftermath of the divorce, Uma noticed a significant change in her parents. Her mother, once known for her perpetual smile and graceful demeanor, had lost weight and seemed to carry the burden of sorrow on her shoulders. Dark circles under her eyes spoke volumes of the sleepless nights spent worrying about her daughter's well being. Even Uma's father, typically stoic and reserved, showed signs of emotional distress. It was a stark reminder of the profound impact that Vishvesh's actions had on their family.

The experience marked a significant turning point in their lives, reshaping their relationships and altering their outlook on the future. Despite the pain and heartache, Uma and her parents remained resilient, drawing strength from each other as they navigated through this challenging chapter in their lives.

Despite Vishvesh's compliance with signing the divorce papers without resistance, the emotional toll on Uma's life was undeniable. She found herself losing interest in the simple joys of life, instead immersing herself in long hours at the office. However, amidst the turmoil, there was a glimmer of hope in Uma's professional success.

Uma's unwavering dedication and hard work had not gone unnoticed in her career. Her commitment and perseverance had yielded significant rewards, with her making notable progress in her professional endeavors. While her personal life may have been in disarray, Uma's achievements in her career served as a source of encouragement and validation during this challenging time.

Seeing Uma lost in her own thoughts, Sarita felt compelled to draw her back into the present conversation. With a direct question, she sought Uma's reaction to her earlier bold statements.

"Are you shocked by my reckless words?" Sarita inquired. "What I say holds truth. Let us weigh the benefits and reach a logical conclusion. Do you truly believe those boys would misbehave with us?"

Uma took a moment to process Sarita's words, trying to recall the context of their discussion. After a brief pause, she responded, "One cannot deny that possibility."

Sarita, undeterred, offered reassurance. "We are not alone; the two of us can handle the situation if it comes to that."

Reluctantly, Uma accepted, "That's true," albeit with a hint of hesitation in her voice.

Reflecting on Sarita's words and her own hesitations, Uma couldn't help but draw parallels to a previous phase in her life when she resided in the Harmony Complex. During that time, she was naive and had yet to experience the harsh realities of the world. In comparison, the level of security she would have in the company of Jagan and Kartik seemed far stronger.

Admitting this to herself, Uma acknowledged the potential benefits of their proposed living arrangement. Despite her reservations, she couldn't ignore the fact that her past experiences had shaped her perceptions and influenced her decision-making process in the present.

"To be honest with you, I have no qualms if we have casual sex with anyone at some sentimental moment, provided we are both willing for it. I won't consider it a sin. It happens. It's but natural. Of course, that's my outlook," shrugging her shoulders, Sarita confided.

Sarita's candid confession left Uma speechless. While she understood that societal views on casual sex were evolving, she couldn't personally reconcile with the idea. Despite being labeled as married and divorced, Uma had yet to experience sexual intimacy. Her own beliefs and values prevented her from engaging in physical relationships without commitment.

Though she recognized the validity of differing opinions, Uma struggled to articulate her thoughts on the matter. Instead, she attempted to deflect with a light hearted remark. "You and your opinions! Everybody has the right to their own perspective. Yet, I must admit, I feel like an old puritan lady talking to you," she said with a smile, avoiding a direct confrontation of their differing views.

Sarita's reasoning gave Uma pause for thought. Despite the potential risks of accepting Jagan's proposition, Uma realized that similar dangers could exist elsewhere. Traveling alone at odd hours on public transport, for example, presented its own set of risks. In essence, Uma recognized that the choice boiled down to two sets of risks, each with its own implications.

Feeling unsettled by these considerations, Uma found herself unable to fully articulate her concerns to Sarita. The complexity of her emotions made it difficult to engage in a meaningful discussion or offer a counterargument. Sensing the impasse, Uma decided to end the conversation and retire to her bed, leaving the matter unresolved for the time being.

As Uma lay awake that night, her mind wandered back to a pivotal moment in her life: her maiden visit to the USA before her wedding to Vishvesh in the year 1999. She recalled the excitement of planning her wedding while simultaneously receiving her first chance to work offshore. It was an opportunity she had eagerly awaited, a chance to experience the western atmosphere of an advanced country like the USA.

On that particular day, however, her plans were unexpectedly interrupted when her boss, Subrahmanyam, urgently summoned her to his cabin. To her surprise, she found Mr. Mehra and Mr. Padukon already present. They had decided to send Uma along with three boys on a three-month project to New York—a prospect that both excited and unnerved her. Despite the inconvenience of the timing, Uma knew she couldn't let this opportunity pass her by.

......

Uma's arrival in freezing January in New York shattered her dreams of a comfortable life abroad. Initially, the company had arranged accommodation for her and the boys in a cheap hotel near the client's office. However, due to her being the only girl on the team, the company couldn't place her in the shared quarters at the company guest house with the boys. Instead, she was left to arrange her own accommodation, with the option of staying with an Indian family if she wished, with reimbursement provided by the company.

Opting to stay with the Mehta's in a distant suburb, Uma found herself facing the challenges of commuting alone in the early mornings, bundled up in warm clothes and shivering at the bus stop on her way to the metro station. Despite managing for a couple of weeks, the prospect of an extended project duration prompted Uma to seek alternative accommodation. Ultimately, she decided to move to a flat near the client's office in the Harmony complex.

Uma found herself in a situation she had never anticipated. The challenges of living alone in a bustling city like New York were overwhelming. She wasn't particularly interested in getting to know her neighbors, but circumstances forced her to take notice of them. Night after night, she was disturbed by the loud music coming from the flat above hers. On weekends, the noise escalated as people indulged in late-night parties, their laughter and clinking glasses echoing through the building. One encounter with a large, imposing man left Uma feeling uneasy, his fierce smile sending her hurrying back to the safety of her own apartment.

Uma's unease grew as the unsettling encounters continued. Accustomed to the solid structures of cement houses in India, the wooden apartment felt flimsy, heightening her sense of vulnerability. Desperate for a roommate, she hastily accepted Mitali's offer without even meeting her in person. However, Mitali abruptly left after just a fortnight, leaving Uma to shoulder the rent alone.

As if that wasn't enough, Uma began receiving disturbing letters slipped under her door, written in an inappropriate language. The letters became increasingly vulgar with each passing day, suggesting that someone was watching her closely. References to her clothing colors and daily routines left Uma feeling exposed and frightened.

Uma found herself trapped in a scenario akin to a horror film. During the final week of her stay, her nightly routine involved barricading the door with heavy furniture and luggage just to ensure a semblance of safety and a decent night's sleep. The constant fear and disruption took a toll on her work performance, affecting its quality and her overall well-being.

Uma, as a matter of principle, never sought special treatment from the company simply because she was female. However, she eventually confided in Chetan Varma, her team lead, about her predicament. Chetan had to intervene and convince the male team members to relocate to Uma's flat, thereby vacating the quarters in the company guest house. This made her feel guilty for inconveniencing them. Indeed, the idea of Uma staying with her male teammates was unprecedented and unexpected for many involved. Traditional norms and societal expectations often dictate separate accommodations for men and women, especially in professional settings.

This situation highlighted the entrenched values and norms ingrained in society over generations. There were rigid and predetermined codes of conduct regarding interactions between men and women, leaving no room for reevaluation or flexibility.

Were we so entrenched in traditional values? Were we not willing to adapt to the changing times, despite women working alongside men in every domain? Uma found herself taken aback by her own words. Why was she reflecting in the past tense? Could it be a sign that she's becoming less rigid in her thinking?

Even now, I find myself investing a considerable amount of time and energy in deliberating the suitability and appropriateness of residing with Jagan and Kartik... What am I fearful of? Why this hesitation? I must evolve and exhibit the courage displayed by Sarita. Let others say what they may, I am indifferent to their opinions.

She rose and positioned herself before the mirror, peering into her own eyes, she repeated, "I couldn't care less! Let them rot!" tossing her head back to adjust the strands of hair cascading on her forehead exactly like Sarita, and giggled. She felt invigorated now. She glanced at her reflection again and affirmed, "Yes, I can do this. I won't be bewildered by the rapid pace of the evolving world any longer. I will immerse myself in the mainstream and align with it. Zannam me gaya Jamana!"

……

Lessons Unlearned

We had recently relocated from our cramped two-room flat in the city to a more spacious apartment on the outskirts. I had hoped that this move would alleviate my daily stresses. The new flat boasted ample space and refreshing cross-ventilation, a welcome change from our previous dwelling. Additionally, we enjoyed the convenience of abundant tap water—a luxury we had longed for. I found solace in the company of our neighbor, Nandini, who was affable and talkative. For us women, these simple comforts were all we desired. However, amidst the excitement of our new surroundings, one crucial aspect had been overlooked.

My sons, Sanju and Manju, were playful yet somewhat reserved. They seemed hesitant to socialize with new acquaintances, often preferring to remain indoors. Encouraging them to go out and mingle with the neighborhood children usually fell on deaf ears. Instead, they would spend their time at home, engaging in trivial arguments. This recurring issue accompanied us through each of my husband's transfers, prompting me to constantly seek inventive ways to involve them in constructive activities.

Our new home, situated far from the bustling township, presented a unique challenge. I grappled with the dilemma of leaving them unattended in an unfamiliar environment. Taking them along for routine errands risked boredom on their part. Despite the abundance of children nearby, I hesitated to suggest they join in their games. Experience had taught me that parental advice often fell on deaf ears when it came to children's preferences.

One day, I received a note from a neighbor named Nalini. Despite our lack of formal introduction, she extended an invitation to her house for the following day at 4 p.m. Curiosity piqued, I found myself at Nalini's place pondering the purpose behind this unexpected gathering, my mind spinning with possibilities.

As I contemplated on my potential excuses, Nalini approached me with a warm smile. "Hello there! I'm so glad you could make it," she greeted me. Her welcoming demeanor caught me off guard, momentarily softening my resolve to find an excuse to leave.

I returned her smile hesitantly. "Thank you for inviting me," I replied politely, still unsure of what was to come.

Nalini gestured for me to take a seat among the group of women. "Please, have a seat. We're just about to start," she said cheerfully.

I complied, feeling a bit apprehensive about what was about to unfold. The other women greeted me with nods and smiles, and I reciprocated, trying my best to mask my unease.

Once everyone was settled, Nalini cleared her throat and addressed the group. "Thank you all for coming today. As you know, we've gathered here to discuss something important," she began, her tone serious yet inviting.

I quickly deduced that the gathering might be centered around the formation of a group for a kitty party or perhaps an invitation for card games. Instantly, I felt a surge of apprehension and began mentally crafting excuses to politely decline. While I had no desire to offend anyone, the prospect of engaging in such frivolous activities held no appeal for me.

The thought of sitting through idle chatter or participating in card games made me inwardly cringe. I couldn't fathom spending my time on activities that held no value or meaning to me. However, I was acutely aware of the need to navigate this situation tactfully, without causing offense to my neighbors.

As I scanned the room, observing the familiar faces engaged in conversation, I silently debated my options. It was clear that I needed to find a diplomatic way to decline their invitation while maintaining cordial relations. After all, I didn't want to risk alienating myself from the community over a difference in interests.

With a sense of determination, I resolved to gracefully extricate myself from the situation, all the while hoping to convey my appreciation for the invitation without committing to something that didn't align with my values or interests.

To my pleasant surprise, Nalini had an entirely different proposal in mind. As it turned out, all the ladies gathered there faced similar challenges when it came to engaging their children in meaningful activities while juggling their daily household responsibilities. With around fifteen to twenty children in the neighborhood, it was a shared concern among us.

Nalini's innovative suggestion instantly caught everyone's attention. She proposed that each of us, belonging to the same age group and with children of similar ages, take turns to organize activities for the children. This would involve dedicating one and a half hours in the evenings once a week to engage the children in games, storytelling, teaching them verses, and imparting valuable life lessons and etiquette.

The designated "lady in charge" for each session would oversee the activities, ensuring that the children were entertained and engaged in constructive pursuits. In turn, this arrangement would allow the other mothers to focus on their household chores or enjoy their leisure activities without the constant worry of supervising the children. It was a brilliant solution that promised to benefit both the children and the mothers alike.

Everyone readily embraced this novel idea, relieved that a solution had been found to their shared dilemma. Together, we selected a suitable location for these classes and designated the days for our respective duties. The following week marked the implementation of this initiative.

Initially, the children were shy and hesitant, but as the sessions progressed, they grew more comfortable with each other and with the designated "lady in charge." They enthusiastically participated in various games, engaging in lively discussions and occasional disagreements, all of which provided valuable learning experiences. By the end of each session, the children eagerly stepped forward to recite verses, share jokes, and narrate stories, showcasing their newfound skills and confidence.

Through this collective effort, not only were the children benefiting from the structured activities, but we as mothers were also forging closer bonds with one another, fostering a sense of community and support within our neighborhood.

On Fridays, it was my turn to engage the children. Langdi, a popular game among them, was always in demand. After the customary prayer, the children eagerly clamored for a round of Langdi. Dividing themselves into two teams, they enthusiastically commenced the game. As the players became fully immersed in the action, I couldn't help but be captivated by their energy and enthusiasm.

However, my attention was soon drawn to two children standing on the sidelines, their eyes fixed intently on the game in progress.

The dark-skinned girl, approximately eight years old, stood beside a younger boy, about five years old, both observing the game with keen interest. The girl's light blue frock, now stained and muddy, draped loosely around her, while tufts of unkempt hair framed her face. The boy's shirt, missing several buttons, hung open, and his over-sized half pants threatened to slip down his waist, which he attempted to secure with his elbows. His bare feet were caked with layers of mud, and dried watermarks adorned his calves. Despite their disheveled appearance, both children radiated joy and excitement, their faces alight with mirth as they silently cheered on the players, urging them to dodge the catcher and run faster. In moments of suspense, they themselves squirmed with anticipation, fully engrossed in the game unfolding before them.

As the players noticed my gaze directed towards the pair, players' attention shifted as well, fixing on the pair standing at the sidelines. Gradually, the entire group began to stare, their collective gaze focusing on the unfamiliar duo. Sensing the scrutiny, the strangers grew uneasy, their expressions betraying a sense of apprehension. Their fearful eyes darted around, seeking refuge from the intense scrutiny. In their anxious search for solace, their gaze eventually settled on me, pleading for reassurance amidst the uncomfortable scrutiny.

Chandu's harsh reprimand pierced the air, his words laden with arrogance as he barked at the children, "What are you doing here? Leave at once!" The fear in those two pairs of innocent eyes was palpable, their vulnerability laid bare by Chandu's callous words.

I didn't want to intimidate them further. With a warm smile, I spoke gently, "Could you tell me your names, please?"

Chandu's response was blunt and insensitive. He interjected before Lati and Kisnya could respond, stating callously, "Their names are Lati and Kisnya. "He further added, "They belong to a lower caste."

I fixed Chandu with a stern gaze and addressed him firmly, without raising my voice, "Chandu, whom did I ask the question? Did I ask about their caste?" My intention was clear: to put Chandu in his place and disapprove of his rude behavior.

I turned my attention back to the strangers and repeated my question. Shyly, they told me their names and smiled timidly.

"Do you like to watch the game?" I asked gently. "It doesn't matter if you stand and watch these boys play." I assured them.

In that week, three of my colleagues were preoccupied with their personal work. Hence, I ended up conducting this class for four consecutive days. With the number of spectators gradually increasing to 6-7, I found myself managing not only our members but also the spectators. They, too, had arguments and fights among themselves. This sparked a splendid idea within me. Overwhelmed with it, I impulsively asked them,

"Would you like to join this group and play with these children?"

They had never expected this question from me, hence didn't know how to react. They just kept mum and started looking at each other. Lati, being the smartest of the lot, replied, "Yes, Madam, we would."

All her friends joined her, and unanimously they said, "Yes, Ma'am."

I laid down certain conditions before letting them join the group.

"You will have to be very clean. You will have to wash your hands and feet, comb your hair like these children. You will have to listen to the Ma'am who is in charge of the group. Is that acceptable? Are you ready to follow the rules?"

They instantly agreed unanimously.

"If you do not listen to the Ma'am, if you use abusive language, or if you are not clean, you will be sent home. Is that clear?" I emphasized in a stern tone.

I asked them to join the next day. I did not question and reconsider the desirability of my own decision till I reached home. As I reflected on my decision while heading home, I realized it was made impulsively, without consulting my colleagues. I assumed that if the children behaved well and maintained cleanliness, my colleagues would have no objections. However, I questioned the wisdom of making this decision on my own. Although none of my colleagues objected, I sensed that some may not have fully embraced the idea.

The children from the slums began joining our group to play and quickly integrated. They quickly grasped our playing techniques and matched our skills with ease. Despite their language skills and pronunciation being lacking, they confidently shared stories and even recited religious verses they had learned at home. It would have been unfair to fault them for their worn-out clothes and send them away. I naively believed that this harmonious arrangement would continue unchanged.

The scene overwhelmed me as I arrived the following Friday. Nearly forty children stood in rows, patiently awaiting the start of our session. Our original group members now seemed outnumbered, standing nervously among the crowd. Meanwhile, Lati and Kisnya had transformed, exuding confidence and leading the group with boldness. I found myself at a loss on how to manage these energetic and lively children, who, though not misbehaving, presented a unique challenge. Indeed, it was an entirely novel experience for them. Despite my efforts to instruct them loudly, my throat soon grew sore, yet even this did not calm their enthusiasm. Games proceeded with difficulty, lacking the usual smoothness.

Next week all the colleagues had a meeting. All attendees shared common challenges in managing the expanded group dynamics. I hadn't anticipated that inviting a small group of slum dwellers to join would result in so many more expressing interest in participating. Bringing in these additional children had disturbed the balance of our group. Our friend Nandini was forthright. She bluntly said,

"We have not started this activity to entertain these slum dwellers. Nor as a social service. We don't want our children to adopt their manners and habits. We should put an end to this immediately."

"How can we stop them? What justification can we provide? We cannot forbid them simply because of their worn-out clothes, can we?" One other friend argued.

Sandhya, the third one, proposed a practical solution. She suggested,

"We can skillfully avoid them. We would be more strict about our rules of personal cleanliness. If we find any child with unkempt hair or dirty feet, we will send them back. Ultimately, they will be discouraged and give up."

We decided to use those tactics. It made me restless. There was something seriously wrong in our outlook. But I could not dare speak out frankly.

Next Friday, I sent Lati back because she had not combed her hair and washed her face. Bajrang had not washed his hands and feet properly, so he too had to be sent home. Lati reappeared within five minutes with combed hair and a washed face. In her eagerness to return quickly, she had applied powder on her damp face, resembling a saint whose face is covered with holy ashes.

Bajrang returned without cleaning his hands and feet, standing in front of me with his head bowed down.

I asked him, "What's the matter?"

He appeared embarrassed, yet he replied, "Mam, tap water is not available."

Now I was a bit annoyed. I raised my voice and said, "If you don't have tap water, why don't you use stored water? You must have a drum full of water. You could have washed with it."

"Mam, we have only one small container at home. Its empty." Bajrang replied awkwardly.

I felt a pang of guilt. My irritation seemed misplaced now. Bajrang's simple explanation made me realize the harsh reality of their living conditions.

Yes, it was a stark reminder of our own ignorance and insensitivity towards the challenges faced by the residents of the slums. It was a humbling moment for me. I couldn't bear to add to Bajrang's embarrassment. I invited him back to join the group, feeling a deep sense of remorse for my earlier actions.

Next week, we convened another meeting to evaluate the effectiveness of our ingenious solution. Sandhya reported that there was a noticeable improvement in the habits of the members due to our stringent measures. We were perplexed. We should have been pleased with this transformation. This transformation was achieved easily and without much difficulty. However, our narrow-mindedness prevented us from recognizing this. All we were focused on was excluding the slum dwellers, no matter what.

I condemned our mindset. I felt deeply saddened by it. Even now, I feel ashamed of our actions. I pondered deeply on the matter, realizing that something was seriously amiss. I found myself questioning our actions: what were we truly doing for those children? Were we sharing the toys belonging to our children with them? Were we offering them snacks and sweets? Did we ever think of purchasing anything for them out of our own pockets? Each of us was dedicating only one hour a week to them. Yet, it brought happiness and meaning to their lives. It was aiding in shaping their personalities and characters. They were being taught cleanliness, language nuances, and correct pronunciations. They were learning etiquette, good manners, and religious verses. Then why were we so miserly and insensitive?

All of us were grooming our own children at home. It was a twenty-four hour duty. Were we not confident in the effectiveness of what our children learned at home? Were we not confident in the strength of the values instilled by us in the minds of our children at home? Then what values were we intending to impart to those children from the slums? Were those values and manners so fragile and easily erasable that they could vanish if our children interacted with those from the slums for just one hour, and that too under our supervision? If that were the case, then what lasting virtues and values could we possibly instill in these children in just one hour? How were we expecting to nurture them? Indeed, our peculiar mindset laid bare the values ingrained in our own characters. Our behavior was a stark reflection of this reality.

I harbored no annoyance toward my friends; rather, I empathized with their psychology. I empathized with their genuine anxiety because I shared their perspective. I, too, belonged to their group and class, and yet I couldn't bring myself to insist that they reconsider their attitude and decision. Yet I could not let the matter end there.

Nalini and I approached a well-known social worker from our locality. We explained the situation to him, highlighting the eagerness of some young slum dwellers to enhance their quality of life through participation in activities like ours. We shared our experiences with him, expressing our challenges in effectively managing the situation. Nalini and I offered to dedicate our time to the activity if he agreed to take over. However, he patiently listened to our plea, smiled, and shook his head in negation.

Indeed, it's an ironic situation. Despite his dedication to social causes, he couldn't spare time for these children in need. We did not want to spare our precious time because we did not want to indulge in social work! Unfortunately, it seems that none of us had either time or empathy for innocent children despite their eagerness to participate and improve their lives..

I had approached this man as a last resort. It was disheartening when efforts to seek help and support did yield no results, especially when the cause was as noble as helping underprivileged children. I alone was responsible for the whole problem. I had asked those children to join the group, on my own. If my team members did not approve of it then it was my moral duty to resolve the matter amicably. And I upheld my responsibility.

One fine evening, I declared in a fake, pretentious affectionate voice..

"From next month onward, everyone will be required to contribute two rupees. We are considering organizing competitions, and with these funds, we will be able to provide snacks and prizes."

That was it! From the next day onward, we were relieved to see our fifteen original members at the ground. We were free to bravely tackle, handle, and groom our own children without fear. I still remember how the earlier day we had conducted a special meeting and shamelessly discussed what would be the exact amount of money that would prohibit them from coming.

Lati, Kisnya and company forgot the temporary phase of discipline and cleanliness in their lives. Once again they resumed their usual life style full of bad words, abusing and filth. I used to see them every day on the road. I used to feel sorry and used to brood over it.

When they saw me on the road, they used to call in their innocent fashion to me 'Mam'. The stark difference between the innocent demeanor of the children and the conniving behavior of the adults was evident in our actions. However, I couldn't bring myself to confess to them that I had long forfeited my right to be called "Mam."

....

Relieved

Niranjan savored the last bite of the ice cream cone his father, Ashvin, had purchased for him from the nearby shop. Perched on the pillion seat of the bike, he cast a grateful smile towards Ashvin.

"Dad, let's head home. Mom must be waiting for us. I won't mention that we went to Grandpa's place and he gave me money for ice cream. Promise! Otherwise, she'll scold us." Niranjan wiped his mouth with the back of his hand as he spoke.

Ashvin shuddered at the prospect of returning home, dreading the potential scene awaiting him. He reached into his pocket, extracting a handkerchief to dab at the sweat on his forehead. Retrieving a comb from his back pocket, he glanced into the bike's mirror and smoothed his hair. Checking his wristwatch, he noted the time: eight thirty PM. Just then, he spotted his neighbors Vishwas and his wife Shubha, likely returning home from their own errands.

"Let's go," said Ashvin, starting the bike with a single kick. Niranjan held onto Ashvin's back from behind, a gesture that always filled Ashvin with joy at the touch of his son's tender palms. He steered the bike out of the community's main gate and paused near Vishwas.

"The other day you mentioned borrowing a DVD from me, right? I've set it aside. If you come with me now, I can give it to you. It won't take long," Ashvin suggested.

"Yes, I'd like to get it now. Since it's the weekend, we can watch it tonight. I'm in the mood for a good movie, buddy! I'll return it by Monday," Vishwas agreed.

Ashvin assured Vishwas. Shubha, on the other hand, left the group, saying, "I have to go now, don't keep me waiting. Come soon."

Ashvin unlocked the door to his flat and stepped inside, with Niranjan and Vishwas trailing behind. The sitting room was cluttered with various items strewn about haphazardly. Ashvin cleared the sofa by removing some laundry to make space. As he headed towards the inner room, he turned to Vishwas and said, "Make yourself at home, I'll be back in a few seconds. Alright?"

Vishwas could hear Ashvin's voice from the bedroom, muttering, "Oh no! Not again."

Moments later, Ashvin rushed out from the bedroom and slumped into a chair. He was sweating profusely, holding his head in both hands. His complexion had turned pale, his expression fraught with distress. Just by observing Ashvin, Vishwas could sense that something was wrong, though he couldn't quite grasp the situation.

"What happened? Why do you look so frightened?" Vishwas inquired, concern evident in his voice.

Ashvin managed to utter only two words, "Ketaki... Ketaki has..."

"What about Ketaki? Is she unwell?" Vishwas interrupted, his concern growing.

"I don't know... She has tried..." Ashvin couldn't finish his sentence, overcome with emotion as he started sobbing.

Just then, Niranjan arrived with a glass of water, but his expression turned to shock as he took in the scene. He stared strangely and accidentally dropped the glass, spilling water onto the carpet, forming a small pool.

"Mummy, Mummy!" Niranjan yelled aloud, starting to rush towards the bedroom.

Ashvin, startled, quickly got up and intercepted Niranjan, grasping his arm firmly and pulling him back. "Please, call Shubha. Let her take him upstairs. Please, buddy," Ashvin pleaded.

"Okay, okay. Or would you prefer me to take him upstairs?" Vishwas offered.

"No, please don't leave me alone. I need you. I need you," Ashvin implored, his voice trembling with fear and desperation.

Immediately, Vishwas dialed Shubha's number from his cell phone, not bothering to respond to her queries. Instead, he guided the sobbing Niranjan to Shubha, who was attempting to enter the flat.

"Could you please take care of him and feed him? Let him sleep at our place tonight. It seems Ketaki isn't well. I'll explain everything later," Vishwas instructed Shubha urgently.

After seeing them off upstairs, Vishwas returned to find Ashvin looking more composed. "I've called Dr. Kate. He'll be here in a few minutes. It seems Ketaki has attempted suicide again," Vishwas was informed, Ashvin's voice heavy with concern.

"Oh God! What are you saying? Did you two have an argument or something?" Ashvin asked, shock evident in his tone.

"Every time I mentioned visiting my Dad, she would get upset. I didn't think it was anything serious. I never imagined she would go this far," Ashvin replied, his voice filled with disbelief and sorrow.

"Should we wait for the doctor to arrive? I mean... how serious is her condition?" Ashvin stumbled over his words, his worry palpable.

Ashvin mumbled, "I don't know," his voice barely audible amidst the turmoil in his mind.

"Shall we call an ambulance? If she gets timely medical treatment then..." Vishwas suggested, his tone laced with uncertainty.

Without hesitation, both men hurried into the bedroom. Ketaki lay motionless on the bed, a pool of blood gathering beneath her left arm. Whitish foam lingered on her parted lips, her gown askew, revealing her bare thighs.

Inadvertently, Ashvin moved to adjust Ketaki's gown, his instinct to help overriding his thoughts. But

Vishwas reacted swiftly, gripping Ashvin's arm firmly and speaking in a solemn voice.

"No, don't touch anything. We will have to inform the police," Vishwas urged, his tone weighted with the gravity of the situation.

A wave of horror washed over Ashvin as he struggled to comprehend the scene before him. Vishwas, though visibly shaken, took charge.

Ketaki's mobile lay abandoned in a corner, tempting Ashvin with the possibility of reaching for it. However, Vishwas anticipated his move and restrained him once more, emphasizing the importance of preserving the scene until the authorities arrived. Taking control of the situation, Vishwas assessed Ketaki's condition. It was evident that she wasn't breathing, prompting Vishwas to prioritize calling the ambulance before Dr. Kate's arrival. With time being of the essence, he swiftly took Ashvin's cell phone and dialed Ketaki's parents, breaking the news to them with a heavy heart.

As Ketaki's parents bombarded him with questions, Vishwas tried to maintain composure and politeness, though it was impossible to address all their queries in the midst of the crisis. Sensing the urgency, he cut the conversation short, focusing on ensuring that help arrived as quickly as possible for Ketaki.

"It's necessary to send Niranjan away for safekeeping before the Patils—Ketaki's parents—arrive here. Otherwise, they might try to take him away from me," Ashvin pleaded urgently, a tone of desperation lacing his voice.

Vishwas considered the urgency in Ashvin's plea. "To whom should we entrust this task? Perhaps your brother or sister, or..."

"I will request my cousin Rahul. Please ask Shubha not to give Niranjan to anyone other than Rahul. Please," Ashvin implored, his concern for his son palpable.

"Okay. Ask Rahul to be quick. Shubha wouldn't be able to hold the fort if people resort to threats and violence. She's not accustomed to such intricate situations," Ashvin reiterated urgently.

Shortly after, the ambulance and Dr. Kate arrived one after the other. The commotion naturally piqued the curiosity of the community members, and they began to gather around, watching the scene unfold with a mixture of concern and intrigue.

Dr. Kate conducted a thorough examination of Ketaki and grimly pronounced her deceased. It was evident that she had inflicted fatal cuts to the veins on her left wrist. An empty bottle of Baygon—an insecticide—lay beneath the bed, indicating that she had also ingested the poisonous substance.

With Ketaki's death confirmed, legal formalities and a postmortem examination became necessary. The body would need to be transferred to the public hospital for police procedures and further investigation into the tragic circumstances surrounding her demise.

Momentarily, Ashvin snapped back to awareness as he registered the threatening words, casting a quick glance at Vishwas for reassurance. With a single blink,

Vishwas confirmed Niranjan's safety. It was all Ashvin needed to find a semblance of reassurance amidst the chaos and turmoil surrounding him.

With the confirmation of Niranjan's safety, a wave of relief washed over Ashvin. His tense shoulders dropped, and his face settled into an expressionless void, a mask to shield himself from the overwhelming emotions threatening to consume him. In that moment of respite, he found a brief refuge from the storm raging within.

The police team swiftly took control of the house, moving around with purpose. Photographers snapped shots from various angles, documenting the scene meticulously. Suddenly, Inspector Nemade emerged from his jeep with his assistants in tow. Holding a stick in one hand, his movements were agile, and the loud sound of his shoes echoed through the room. His crisp demeanor commanded respect and awe, instilling a sense of authority in all who beheld him.

As Inspector Nemade made his entrance, Ashvin's first impression was one of apprehension. The police team's swift movements and the inspector's commanding presence instilled a sense of unease within him. Inspector Nemade's agile demeanor, coupled with the crisp sound of his shoes, evoked a feeling of authority that left Ashvin feeling small in comparison.

Standing at a formidable six feet tall, Inspector Nemade's stout and muscular frame, along with his dark complexion and piercing brown eyes, lent him a commanding presence. The tufts of his mustache added to his imposing appearance, while his glances seemed to drill into the surroundings, leaving no detail unnoticed.

Despite not displaying any overt fierceness or arrogance, Inspector Nemade's mere presence filled Ashvin with apprehension. He knew that the inspector was unlikely to miss any minute detail, further intensifying his unease.

Despite knowing he had nothing to hide from Inspector Nemade or anyone else, Ashvin couldn't shake off his apprehension. "I haven't done anything wrong," he reassured himself, but the need to be cautious and attentive persisted. He understood the unpredictability of police investigations and the potential for innocuous statements to be twisted into incriminating evidence. As Inspector Nemade approached, Ashvin's mind raced with possibilities. What if he asked probing questions or fixated on insignificant details? Ashvin felt a pang of guilt for his apprehension; after all, he hadn't violated any laws. Yet, the mere presence of the inspector stirred a sense of unease within him.

Confronting Inspector Nemade, Ashvin would likely feel a mix of anxiety and frustration. Despite his innocence, the fear of being misunderstood or falsely accused would weigh heavily on him. He might find himself second-guessing every word he utters, wary of inadvertently incriminating himself. The realization that even the innocent could be ensnared in the complexities of the law would only heighten his apprehension and discomfort.

As Inspector Nemade's presence loomed, Ashvin's mind wandered, drawn to the countless Marathi and English stories he had devoured over the years. In those tales, he had encountered protagonists navigating through similar predicaments—innocent yet entangled in the web of suspicion and intrigue. Recollections of characters facing unjust accusations and navigating treacherous interrogations flooded Ashvin's thoughts. He remembered their struggles to maintain their innocence in the face of relentless scrutiny, their words dissected and twisted by those in authority.

In those stories, Ashvin had found solace and reassurance, learning from the protagonists' resilience and determination to prevail against adversity. Yet, as he stood before Inspector Nemade, he couldn't help but feel a twinge of uncertainty, unsure if his own story would unfold with the same fortitude and resolve.

Inspector Nemade meticulously combed through every room of Ashvin's modest dwelling, his keen eyes scrutinizing every detail. From the furniture arrangement to the scattered items strewn about, nothing escaped his observation. He took note of Ketaki's cell phone, the empty bottle of insecticide, and even the creases on the bed sheet.

Bombarding his assistants with instructions, Inspector Nemade directed their efforts with precision. He advised the official photographers on the angles to capture, ensuring every aspect of the scene was documented thoroughly. With gloved hands, he delicately lifted Ketaki's cell phone, sealing it in a thin poly bag for further analysis.

As Ashvin became increasingly detached from the commotion around him, Inspector Nemade approached and stood before him. With a solemn expression, Inspector Nemade addressed Ashvin, acknowledging the gravity of the situation.

"It is a very sad incidence. I can very well imagine how difficult it could be for you," Inspector Nemade began, his tone formal yet tinged with a hint of consideration. "I do not wish to bother you, but I am left with no choice. I have to perform my duty and complete the formalities."

Despite his attempt at showing consideration, Inspector Nemade's voice remained devoid of empathy, reflecting the official courtesy expected in such circumstances. It was a stark reminder to Ashvin that, amidst the personal tragedy, the wheels of bureaucracy continued to turn without pause.

"I totally agree with you. You have to perform your duty. But I am very much confused... I would cooperate with you, I promise," Ashvin replied, his voice tinged with uncertainty.

"We would have to talk leisurely. We will meet in my office tomorrow. Nobody would disturb us there," Inspector Nemade stated, lifting his left eyebrow in a gesture prompting Ashvin's affirmative reply. Without waiting for a response, he moved towards the door.

Ashvin had no choice but to cooperate, and both were aware of this fact. The next day, in Inspector Nemade's office, cups of strong tea were ordered. As they settled in, Inspector Nemade began with the factual information—name, age, education, job, and so forth. Before delving into Ketaki's case, he smiled apologetically, breaking the tension.

As the preliminary details were covered, a hotel boy appeared with two glasses of tea, bringing a sense of relaxation to Ashvin. His initial apprehensions began to dissipate, and he surmised that Inspector Nemade's habit of lifting his left eyebrow was simply part of his style, without any deeper implications.

Ashvin had barely taken a few sips of tea when Inspector Nemade broached the topic. "Now we will talk about yesterday's incidence. Tell me everything as it happened. Begin with the beginning. What did you see when you entered the house?"

"Vishwas, Niranjan—my son—and I entered the house. I had met Vishwas on my way home. I had promised to lend him a DVD. As we entered the..."

"Didn't you ring the doorbell?" Inspector Nemade interjected.

"No. I never ring the doorbell. It is never felt necessary. Ketaki and I have separate sets of keys. Ketaki is often busy. Sometimes she is not at home. Hence..."

Ashvin's apprehension grew after his response. "Am I replying as if I have rehearsed it and know it by heart?" he wondered. However, Inspector Nemade seemed unperturbed and urged him to continue.

"I see... Go ahead. You were narrating the course of events after entering the house," Inspector Nemade prompted, keeping the conversation flowing smoothly.

Ashvin heaved a sigh of relief, reminding himself, "I haven't done anything." Gathering his composure, he took a deep breath and began to recount the events.

"I asked Vishwas to have a seat in the drawing room and went into the bedroom. There, I found Ketaki lying in bed. I could see a pool of blood under her left arm, and her lips were covered with whitish foam. I was shocked to see her condition," Ashvin's voice trembled as he narrated Ketaki's distressing state. His facial muscles tensed, and his eyes glistened with emotion, reflecting the turmoil within him.

"When you saw her condition, what was your immediate reaction? Did you do anything since you were in shock?" Inspector Nemade inquired.

"I didn't do anything. I hurried to the drawing room," Ashvin replied.

"Why didn't you call her name or try to awaken her? That would have been the natural reaction in such a situation," the inspector pressed further.

Ashvin paused to recollect. "Why didn't I try to awaken her?" After a moment, he replied, "It didn't occur to me. I was scared. I was nervous. Her posture wasn't normal. It was obvious she had stopped breathing."

"You're not a doctor by profession, right?" Inspector Nemade questioned.

"No. I'm an engineer. I didn't notice it. It was Vishwas who noticed it first," Ashvin replied.

"How?" the inspector inquired.

"He called the ambulance. Later, we scrutinized the scene," Ashvin explained.

"Did you touch anything? Or shift anything from the initial place?" Inspector Nemade continued.

"No," Ashvin replied.

"Why not? Hadn't you already suspected that she was dead?" the inspector probed.

"No. In fact, I tried to adjust Ketaki's gown. Her thighs were exposed. Vishwas cautioned me not to touch anything," Ashvin clarified.

"So, you didn't touch anything after that, right? But how did Vishwas know that something was amiss in the bedroom? You had made him sit in the drawing room, isn't it?" the inspector questioned further.

Ashvin paused, trying to recollect the sequence of events. "Yes," he finally confirmed.

"Now listen to my questions carefully and then answer. What did you do after seeing Ketaki's condition?" Inspector Nemade directed, signaling the beginning of the interrogation.

"My head started spinning. I rushed to the drawing room and collapsed on the sofa. Vishwas surmised that something had gone wrong... At least, that is what I think. He came near me and started inquiring. At that moment, I started sobbing," Ashvin recounted.

"What happened next?" Inspector Nemade prompted.

"Niranjan panicked and was about to rush to the scene of... tragedy... I stopped him. There was no need for Niranjan to witness it, that's what I thought," Ashvin continued, his voice laden with emotion as he recalled the distressing events.

"Till then, where was Niranjan?" Inspector Nemade questioned.

"He was in the kitchen. He was fetching a glass of water for Vishwas. He came with a glass of water and saw me in that condition," Ashvin replied, attempting to evade Inspector Nemade's piercing gaze.

"It seems you have groomed your son well..." Inspector Nemade remarked.

Ashvin couldn't comprehend the meaning behind this remark, appearing perplexed.

"He went to fetch a glass of water for the guest... nice etiquette," Inspector Nemade explained, without averting his gaze from Ashvin's quizzical expression.

Ashvin didn't comment. Instead, he lifted a glass of water and drank a couple of sips before continuing, "I made a call to Dr. Kate. No, wait... I asked Vishwas to send Niranjan to Vishwas's home upstairs. You may ask Vishwas about it."

Inspector Nemade was about to ask a question but decided otherwise. He scribbled something down on his notepad before posing another inquiry, "Why didn't you call the ambulance before calling the doctor?"

Ashvin, feeling exhausted, grew irritated and replied, "I have already told you that I was not in a proper frame of mind."

"Did you have a fight earlier that afternoon? Any serious arguments?" Inspector Nemade pressed further.

"Um... Yes. My dad doesn't keep well. I, along with Niranjan, had gone to see him... Ketaki never liked my visiting my own parents. She never liked Niranjan to go with me. Dad was very keen on meeting his grandson. So, that was it. That became the cause of our arguments," Ashvin explained, revealing the tension within his household.

"Where were you when Ketaki attempted suicide?" Inspector Nemade inquired.

"I don't have any idea when she... did this... Maybe I was on my way to Dad's home... Maybe at his residence... I'm not sure. Somewhere between the time I left the home and returned in the evening. I did not go elsewhere," Ashvin responded.

Inspector Nemade noted down a few lines in his notebook. Reading the call register on Ketaki's cell phone, he asked, "Where were you when you received her first call?"

"Please tell me the time," asked Ashvin.

"At 2:35 pm. This call lasted for 2 minutes," Inspector Nemade specified.

"I was in the shop, purchasing sweets for the parents," Ashvin recalled.

"What did you converse?" the inspector probed.

"She urged me not to take Niranjan with me. She also cautioned me that the consequences would be miserable... and so on," Ashvin replied.

"Did she punctuate the details of those said 'miserable consequences'?" Inspector Nemade further inquired.

To Inspector Nemade's utter surprise, Ashvin giggled aloud, leaving him perplexed by this unexpected reaction. Noticing Inspector Nemade's expression, Ashvin quickly came to his senses.

"Sorry, Inspector. I laughed because this was a usual threat from Ketaki. She did not talk to me for weeks. Or as a punishment to me, she used to beat Niranjan. She wouldn't cook for days, didn't let me come near her or touch her. She used to invent new ways to harass me," Ashvin explained, shedding light on the toxic dynamics of his relationship with Ketaki.

"Does it mean that you did not take her threat seriously? She called you again at 2:55. This call lasted for twenty-five minutes. What was the discussion about?" Inspector Nemade questioned.

"Our conversation used to revolve around the same topics. Her standard allegation was that my parents did not treat her well. Every time we had a difference of opinion, she would start hammering the same old allegations. Naturally, I would lose control, and then I would call names. How was I to know that this time something serious would happen?" Ashvin explained.

"Earlier, she had already attempted suicide. Then how come you did not surmise it this time?" Inspector Nemade probed further.

Ashvin was taken aback. He sensed that Inspector Nemade had collected a lot of information in a very short time. "Is he aware of the fact that I and my parents were summoned by the police?" he pondered, feeling a sense of unease at the depth of Inspector Nemade's knowledge.

Taking some time to reply, Ashvin finally spoke up. "That's true. But it was altogether a different case. We had a joint family, and we were staying with my parents. She wanted me to leave that house and make a separate home for us. I didn't wish to leave my parents when they needed me the most. That's why she used such tantrums. But now we have a separate house. Everything is according to her wishes."

"What did she do back then? Did she use insecticide?" Inspector Nemade inquired.

"You must be knowing the answer, then why ask me? You have already gathered information about us... Then why ask me? She did not drink insecticide at the time. She tried to cut her veins on the wrist," Ashvin responded, feeling a sense of frustration at the repetition of questions when the answers seemed evident.

It was evident to both Ashvin and Inspector Nemade that Ashvin was losing control and becoming increasingly irritated. All the same Inspector Nemade continued.

"Okay. Then what did you do then?"

"I dressed her wound at home. The wound was shallow and there was no profuse bleeding. Yet I took her to the doctor. She went into the nearby police station and lodged a complaint against three of us," Ashvin replied, his voice betraying his emotional turmoil.

Ashvin's face distorted with pain, and his eyes glistened with unshed tears, indicating the depth of his emotional distress.

"What do you mean? Are you suggesting that she deliberately inflicted herself with a shallow wound and tried to blackmail you emotionally?" Inspector Nemade probed.

"Please don't put words in my mouth. I never said so," replied Ashvin, with a special emphasis on the word 'I'.

Again, Nemade noted down a few words in his notebook and continued, "After the incident, you made a separate home for you and shifted there for good?"

"My parents panicked. There was not a single embarrassing incident like this in the history of our whole family. I did not wish to separate from Ketaki. Ours was a love marriage. It was very painful for me to leave my parents; they had sacrificed a lot for my upbringing. We had experienced extreme poverty. Both Ketaki and my parents could not tolerate even the sight of each other. That's why..."

"Okay. Let us go back to yesterday's sequence of events. Where were you when you received this 2:55 pm call?"

"I was at my parents' place. I told Dad that the call was from my office and went to the balcony to speak with Ketaki."

"Even after this call, it seems Ketaki tried to contact you thrice; at 3:20 pm, then again at 3:23 pm, and again at 3:37 pm from this phone. It is registered in the phone call history. The duration of calls was short, but you did receive those calls. What happened during those calls?"

Ashvin closed his eyes and tried to recollect. Unknowingly, he nodded twice in negation. Opening his eyes, he said, "Nothing new happened. The repetition of the same dialogues and same arguments..."

"Are you certain? Had she indicated her intention to commit suicide? Take your time, try to remember, and then tell me," Inspector Nemade prompted.

Nemade had a momentary feeling that Ashvin had tried to avoid meeting his staring eyes. Next moment, Ashvin looked at Nemade without a blink and replied, "No, she did not say anything to that effect. I was not in the mood to continue the same conversation again and again. I made it very clear by telling her, 'I am not interested in talking to you unless there is any new topic to discuss.' Then I cut the call and switched it off."

"Does this mean that you were not at all aware of the turmoil in her mind? She had called you seven times within 15 to 20 minutes thereafter. It indicates that there was some urgency," Nemade's stern eyes seemed to drill into Ashvin's.

"How was I to guess? My phone was switched off," Ashvin explained.

Suddenly changing the topic, Nemade probed, "Where did you meet Vishwas?"

Ashvin was perplexed by this sudden change of topic.

"While entering the community main gate, we came across Vishwas and his wife, Shubha," Ashvin explained.

"I see..." Nemade's non-committal remark left Ashvin guessing. He couldn't surmise anything from it, nor could he predict what was to come next. He was at a loss to understand the direction of the queries. Wasn't it a clear-cut suicide case? Then why was Nemade grilling him as if he were a culprit and Nemade a prosecution lawyer cross-examining him in court?

Feeling the pressure, Ashvin pulled out a handkerchief from his pocket and wiped his face, trying to collect his thoughts amidst the intensity of the interrogation.

Ashvin asked Inspector Nemade, "Shall I ask you a question? Why are you asking me these questions? Ketaki resorted to some rash action; how am I held responsible for Ketaki's atrocity?"

"This is a routine procedure. We have to go through every minute detail. Again... Your father-in-law came to the police station to express his doubts about your role in this action. You have already admitted that Ketaki had lodged a complaint against you a couple of years back. Hence..." Nemade shrugged his shoulders to indicate his indifference to accusing Ashvin.

"Inspector, I have done nothing to her. Imagine yourself in my position. If your sick, aged father were craving to see his grandson, what would you have done? You too would have taken your son to meet his grandfather, right? If you have any reservations and doubts about me, you may ask Niranjan. He was with me all the time. But... No, I don't want him to be involved in this matter," Ashvin asserted.

"Relax, buddy. I know it. I will not involve the kid unless it becomes inevitable. I am just doing my duty, nothing else. So far, we have not accused you of anything. At least, not till now. I'm just collecting information from you, understood? So, relax. At what time did you return home?"

"Maybe around quarter past eight. Give or take a few minutes. Vishwas and Shubha may be able to tell you the exact time."

"Your father stays in Pashan. How much time do you usually take to travel on your bike from there to your home in Bibvewadi?"

"In normal circumstances, if there is no traffic rush, I can reach in an hour."

"Yesterday, at what time did you start from Pashan to return home?"

"Wait a minute. Niranjan was watching Pogo or some other cartoon show. We left my parents' house just after the program was over. So it must have been around five forty-five, max "

"Was there a traffic jam or traffic rush? You took ninety minutes from the time you left."

"Five-forty five is a peak hour, right? Then there was a procession on the road. Again, we halted for an ice cream cone. Some time was spent there," calculated Ashvin.

"Where did you halt?"

"We did not go to a restaurant but purchased a cone from a vendor, and Niranjan consumed it on the road itself."

"In which locality were you then?

"We were in Bibvewadi, opposite our house at Ghatge Super Market. My father had given Niranjan some cash to have a cone of ice cream."

"You were near the house; then why did you not carry the cone and let Niranjan eat it in the house? Why wait there?

Ashvin was annoyed with Nemade. Why should he bother about it? My son will eat his cone anywhere he likes. Why is he interfering in our privacy?

"What difference does it make? Ketaki would not have let him eat in peace. She would have scolded Niranjan and quarreled with me. I wished that he should enjoy eating before the tantrums start..... I am answering all your questions patiently.. Why ask such meaningless questions to me?"

"You are not favoring me by replying. In a couple of days, you might be harassed by even stranger and accusing questions by the Prosecution when it comes to face the court trial. Then only you would give straight replies without grumbling."

Ashvin was scared. Court trial? Because Ketaki committed suicide? He mused.

"Sorry, I was out of my mind."

"Could you see the main gate of your community from the spot you were standing?"

"Ghatge Super Market is diagonally opposite to the main gate."

"Which means you could watch the main gate from there?"

"Um… Yes.."

"Which means you saw Vishwas entering through the main gate?"

"I was not aware and did not see him. Is it so important?"

"If you were attentive then you would have seen him, right?"

"But I did not see him because I was not attentive."

"Suppose your seeing Vishwas from the spot is not important then why is it that you are insisting that you had not seen him?"

"I am not insisting but telling you the truth, that's all," Ashvin replied.

Nemade's phone rang suddenly, prompting him to leave abruptly. The inquiry session ended there, with him expressing his intention to continue in the next couple of days. Restless, Ashvin returned home, unable to understand what more there was to discuss. He couldn't fathom why Nemade hadn't simply talked to Dr. Kate to gather all the necessary information. After all, it was Dr. Kate who had declared Ketaki dead, not Ashvin or Vishwas.

Two days passed without any new development. Ashvin was annoyed when Insp. Nemade appeared on the third day with a warrant. How could they take me into custody when it's a case of suicide? Suicide is a legal offense, but what happens if the culprit is already dead? What could be the legal punishment for a dead person? It's unjust to arrest the closest relative of the deceased in such cases, he mused.

"I've told you everything I know. I wasn't anywhere near Ketaki when she attempted suicide, and you're aware of it. How can you arrest me based on somebody's complaint?"

"I know what I can do and what your rights are. I have a warrant with me. Your father-in-law has strong suspicions that you instigated her to commit suicide."

"He can't make such flimsy allegations. You know the facts."

"I know what you've told me, but not necessarily what actually happened. You can argue about it at the police station. I can't do anything more than this. Please let me do my duty. One thing I must tell you: you can have a lawyer present. Anything you say will be held as evidence against you. You're free to call a lawyer immediately." Nemade tried to maintain a polite tone, as any police officer would while on duty.

Ashvin didn't know any lawyers. It had never felt necessary until now. He didn't know whom to turn to for wise advice. He dreaded publicity and hence decided to go with Insp. Nemade without any ado. He collected all the cash in the house, just in case it would be necessary. He made sure to bring his cell phone along. Everything he didn't want to happen had already happened. He didn't want his Dad to know about the incident, but now it seemed inevitable. He called Rahul to check on Niranjan's mental, psychological, and physical condition. It seemed Niranjan was well taken care of at Rahul's place, which was a great relief. Later, Ashvin disclosed the news of his arrest to Rahul. While speaking to Rahul, he was reminded of his colleague, Mr. Rane. He was a knowledgeable person and had acquaintances in all facets of life.

"Please call Mr. Rane from my office and tell him about all the developments. I'm sharing Rane's number with you. Please don't let Dad know about this latest development," he urged.

Nemade didn't seem to be listening to the telephonic conversation between Ashvin and Rahul. Yet Ashvin knew that he must be attentive and grasping every word uttered by him. After reaching the police station, the inquiry began. This time, Nemade didn't feel it necessary to be polite and follow the decorum. He issued a couple of instructions to his subordinates and then turned to Ashvin.

Ashvin guessed that it was Nemade's way of indicating that Ashvin was an accused and a potential culprit. Is he going to accuse me of murder just because Bapu made those allegations? How can he ignore the fact that I was far away from the place of the accident? Before resuming the inquiry, Nemade asked for Ashvin's fingerprints. Then the drill began. Ashvin replied, but all the time he was wondering, how come Nemade is not tired of asking the same questions again and again.

"When did you reach home?" Nemade asked.

"I have already answered all your questions. You have noted down everything in your notebook. Then why ask me again and again?" Ashvin retorted.

"You are not to question me; you have to reply to every question I ask."

Just then Rahul arrived with Mr. Rane and an unknown person who looked like a lawyer.

"Meet Ad. Avhad. He is going to plead Ashvin's case," declared Mr. Rane authoritatively, introducing him to Nemade and Ashvin.

Ad Avhad and Insp. Nemade knew each other. Rahul offered to pay bail, and thereafter, things proceeded smoothly.

Later on, Nemade briefed Ad Avhad on the situation. The Patils had lodged a strong complaint against Ashvin. They had high-level connections with powerful politicians and attempted to intimidate the police officer. They claimed that Ashvin had made Ketaki's life miserable, often arguing with her, physically abusing her, and using vulgar language. Mai, Ketaki's mother, went as far as to suggest that Ashvin may have actually murdered Ketaki and staged it to look like a suicide. The Patils continued to accuse not only Ashvin but also the police department of being deliberately negligent in their investigation. Eventually, the police had to register an FIR against Ashvin for instigating Ketaki's suicide.

.....

Ashvin arrived at the court accompanied by Ad Avhad. He felt relieved to see that the courtroom was not overcrowded. He spotted Mr. Rane and Rahul seated in the third row. Mr. Rane smiled reassuringly at him, while Rahul gave him a thumbs-up sign. In the second row, just in front of Rahul and Rane, Ashvin noticed Mai and Bapu. Mai cast a malicious glance at Ashvin and muttered something to Bapu. At that moment, the judge entered the room, and everyone in the courtroom stood up.

Ad Mandake appeared to be middle-aged, nearing fifty. His salt-and-pepper hair suited him, lending him a dignified appearance. His broad-rimmed glasses complemented his overall look. Despite his dark complexion, his light gray eyes conveyed a sense of gravity. As the prosecutor, he commenced his opening statement in the case between Ashvin and the State.

He began narrating: On the seventeenth day of this month, the police were summoned to Ashvin Shelke's flat in Bibvewadi. Upon arrival, Ketaki Shelke was already deceased. He detailed Ketaki's position upon discovery, the findings of the postmortem report, and the forensic department's analysis, which concluded that her death resulted from insecticide consumption.

Highlighting differences in the Shelkes' relationship, he referenced a heated argument between them on the day of the incident. Indeed, while the evidence suggests suicide, Ketaki's parents have voiced their doubts and suspicions regarding the circumstances of her death. The prosecution aims to explore whether Ashvin played a role in her death. Questions arise: Was Ashvin truly absent from the scene? If it was suicide, could Ashvin have contributed to Ketaki's fatal actions? These are inquiries the prosecution seeks to address. Following his opening statement, the prosecutor began calling witnesses, one after another, to the witness stand.

The first witness called to the stand was Inspector Nemade, who described the scene of the incident in detail and submitted photographs taken by police photographers.

Following him, Dr. Rangnekar, who conducted the postmortem, took the stand. His testimony delved into technicalities, as the deceased had both cut her veins and consumed insecticide. Dr. Rangnekar explained the procedures he followed to determine the cause of death. He noted that there were no traces of insecticide in the blood pool, indicating that death occurred before the poison took effect. Despite the blood loss not being sufficient to cause death, the ingestion of insecticide was deemed the primary cause. Dr. Rangnekar also discussed the effects of the poison on various bodily systems and organs, ultimately concluding that insecticide poisoning was the leading cause of death.

Ad. Avhad conducted the cross-examination of Dr. Rangnekar.

"What is your learned opinion about the quantity of poison consumed by the deceased?" he inquired.

"500 ml of insecticide was found in the bowels of the deceased," Dr. Rangnekar responded.

"How long does it usually take to cause death in such a case?" Avhad inquired further.

"If the person is healthy, it would take 5 to 6 hours," Dr. Rangnekar replied.

"What about a weak and feeble person?" Avhad pressed on.

"After pondering for a few seconds," Rangnekar replied, "Four hours to four and a half hours approximately."

"In this case, the deceased had lost blood before consuming the poison. Suppose the victim is weak and had lost blood... then how much time would be required to cause death? Would it be less than four hours?" asked Ad Avhad.

"It's possible, but one would not be able to tell the exact time," Rangnekar answered.

"Were you aware of Dr. Kate's diagnosis about the probable cause of death?" Avhad inquired.

"Yes, the hospital staff was already informed by the police. However, I examined the body and drew my own conclusion," Rangnekar clarified.

"Were you on duty when the body was brought to the hospital?" Avhad probed.

"Yes, I was on duty, although I was about to leave," Rangnekar confirmed.

"Did you check the body immediately after being admitted?" Avhad questioned further.

"Yes," Rangnekar responded.

"Was she dead? For how long could she have been dead? Can you determine it from the body temperature?" Avhad continued.

"The body temperature was just below 95 degrees. So... not much time had passed," Rangnekar concluded.

"It means that my client was far away from the scene when the sad incident took place, right? The deceased consumed poison and was already dead before my client reached the scene. Can we safely conclude it?" Avhad pressed on.

Rangnekar was about to reply when Ad Mandake swiftly raised an objection, stating, "I object, Your Honor. He is not eligible to express expertise on this matter."

The judge upheld the objection, and Ad Avhad nodded, though a smile lingered on his face. It was clear he had made his intended point for both the judge and the audience to note.

Ignoring the objection, Ad Avhad continued, "Could you determine the time of consumption of the insecticide?"

"Yes, we know what she had for lunch. Taking into consideration the contents of the bowels, we can conclude that she must not have consumed it within 2 hours after lunch," Rangnekar explained.

"What are the chances that she could have consumed it before that?" Ad Avhad inquired further.

"According to my calculations, this conclusion would be 99.66 percent correct. One cannot draw a 100 percent conclusion in such cases," Rangnekar responded.

"Which means that there are absolutely no chances that the poison was consumed before lunch or within 2 hours of lunch. Are you sure about it?" Avhad questioned.

"Yes, one hundred percent," Rangnekar affirmed.

Ad Avhad then declared that the cross-examination was over. Turning to the judge, he pleaded, "My Lord, my client Ashvin Shelke left his Bibvewadi residence around 1:45. Before that, the trio had lunch together. Ashvin was accompanied by his son Niranjan. My client reached home at 8:30 pm. The deceased cut the veins on her wrist, consumed the poison, and died somewhere between 1:45 and 8:30 pm. My client was nowhere near the scene of the incident during this period."

He further continued, "Your Honor, I appreciate the prosecution's diligence in presenting their case. However, I must emphasize that the allegations against my client are baseless and driven by malice. As I mentioned earlier, we have evidence from witnesses such as the housemaid and the courier boy, who can attest to my client's whereabouts during the time of the incident. These testimonies will corroborate the fact that my client was not present at the scene when the tragic events unfolded."

Ad Avhad's rebuttal aimed to highlight the importance of evidence and to discredit any attempts to tarnish his client's reputation with unfounded accusations.

Again Ad Mandake sprang up and said,

"The parents of the deceased have claimed that this was not the first instance of Ashvin instigating the deceased for suicide. This has happened a couple of times before, they have claimed. The accused was summoned to the local police stations and given warning by them."

Ad Avhad swiftly rose to address the judge and the court.

"Your Honor, the prosecution's assertions are mere allegations unsupported by concrete evidence. The claims made by the parents of the deceased lack substantiation and rely solely on hearsay. Furthermore, summoning my client to the local police station and issuing warnings do not prove guilt nor establish a pattern of behavior. Without credible evidence, these allegations remain unfounded and should not influence the court's judgment."

Ad Avhad's response aimed to discredit the prosecution's claims and underscore the importance of tangible evidence in legal proceedings.

Besides he claimed that it was a very old case. He reasoned that if they were genuinely concerned about their daughter's well-being, they would have taken steps to protect her from further harm, such as inviting her to stay with them. By pointing out this inconsistency, Ad Avhad aimed to cast doubt on the credibility of the prosecution's assertions and emphasize the weakness of their case.

Ad Mandake's request to summon more witnesses indicated his intention to bolster the prosecution's case with additional testimony. This move suggested that he believed these witnesses could provide further evidence or testimony to strengthen the prosecution's argument against Ashvin. The judge's approval allowed Ad Mandake to proceed with his plan to present more evidence in court.

Mr. Patil's testimony painted a grim picture of Ashvin's behavior towards Ketaki, alleging emotional harassment, cursing, and abuse. His statement implied that Ketaki endured these conditions due to concern for Niranjan's welfare. This testimony aimed to bolster the prosecution's argument that Ashvin's mistreatment led to Ketaki's distress and eventual suicide.

Ad Avhad probed, "Let us see what happened four years back. During the month of May 2007 and again during October 2008, Ketaki had left her husband's home and gone to stay with you. Every time her stay was for around 60 to 70 days. Why did she find it necessary to return to her husband's home?"

Mr. Patil Paused for a few seconds and replied, "Well, Ketaki... She... She wanted to give her marriage another chance. And we thought... it was best for Niranjan's well-being."

Staring hard at Patil Ad Avhad asked further, "So, despite any issues she may have faced, Ketaki chose to return to her husband's home on those occasions?"

Looking ill at ease and glancing at his wife and then at Ad Mandake, glistening his lips with the tip of his tongue Mr Patil stuttered in a low voice, "Yes, that's correct. Actually they did not have any differences of opinion then."

Ad Avhad paused for a moment, seemingly surprised.

"So, she had come to stay with her parents as is customary in India, to relax and rest, that's all. And eventually, she returned to her home," explained Mr. Patil."Ketaki used to complain about the fights between her and Ashvin, and hence we thought the complaints held truth," he continued.

"And still you let her go back? Or you too were convinced that the fault lay with your daughter?" Patil kept quiet. Avhad did not press for a reply.

Instead, he picked up a cell phone lying in front of him on the table and said, "Here are a few messages which Ketaki had sent to Ashvin, my client, during that period." He then proceeded to read aloud some messages from the phone. In those messages, for the first few days, Ketaki had sent 4-5 messages daily, and her language was aggressive and quarrelsome.

She had not only used abusive language towards Ashvin but also employed derogatory words for his parents. Additionally, she threatened to gain custody of Niranjan and separate him from Ashvin and his parents. Later, her language shifted to complaints not only about her brother and sister-in-law but also about Bapu and Mai. This indicated her temperament and behavior, showing she was not getting along well with her family members.

In the next message, she had raised doubts about Ashvin's friendship with one of his colleagues, Sharmila. She also declared that she was coming back and ordered (not requested) Ashvin to buy groceries. Mr. Patil had no courage to speak further. Avhad placed a printout of these messages on the judge's table. The judge borrowed the phone for a few minutes. After verification Avhad continued, "It is clear from these messages that she could not get along with even her blood relations. She had skirmishes with them too, and after that, she used to come back to her spouse. It proves that Patil's allegations are baseless and indicate vengeance."

Later, Ad Mandake summoned Mr. Ghangurde and Vishwas Rele, who stayed in the flats just above Ashvin's flat in Bibvewadi. Judging from their body language, both of them seemed reluctant to cooperate. Both admitted to the presence of arguments between the couple, noting that they frequently heard their heated voices. But to extract these answers from the duo, Ad Mandake had to pose a series of questions. They also mentioned observing Ashvin and Ketaki riding on Ashvin's bike along with their son.

After Vishwas Rele finished his testimony and left the witness box, Insp. Nemade approached Ad Mandake and discussed something with him in a hushed voice, following which Mandake summoned Ashvin to the witness box for testimony.

Mandake probed, "A few minutes back my lawyer friend Ad Avhad presented a record of some saved messages sent by the deceased to the accused in 2008. When were those messages sent to you by her?"

"I cannot tell you the exact date, but it was somewhere in October or November."

"How many SMS do you send in a day?"

"Do you mean messages to Ketaki?"

"Not to anybody specific, but the total number of SMS per day?"

"Maybe seven to eight... sometimes even ten."

"Do you save all the messages?"

"No. I make it a point to save the important ones."

"Do you consider these messages to be so important so as to save them for years?"

An incredulous and mischievous smile lingered on Ashvin's face. He jokingly replied, "These messages become handy at times of next arguments."

"But these messages are almost two and a half or rather three years old. Were these saved to be used in the future in the court from the witness stand? Try to recollect and then reply."

It was a direct allegation that it was part of a planned strategy to save those and then present them at the right time as proofs against the deceased in the future.

It meant that Mandake proposed to prove it as a preconceived plan of action. The Judge and even Ad

Mandake expected Avhad to raise an objection to such a statement. But he didn't.

"No, I don't have to recollect. This old phone was lying in my cupboard unused. For the last two and a half years, nobody has even touched it. So I did not bother to delete messages from it, that's all," Ashvin clarified confidently.

Mandke's strategy had backfired on him. He wiped sweat from his forehead, removed his glasses, and cleaned them with a cloth.

"I see," Mandake said noncommittally and continued, "We will now try to recollect the sequence of events on the day of the tragic incident."

He asked Ashvin the same questions as Nemade and received the same replies from Ashvin.

"You wife's first call came in to you at 2.35 and you had an argument, that's what you have said. Had she expressed her intention to commit suicide then?"

"No, She was upset, but she didn't mention anything about suicide." Ashvin replied.

Mandake glanced at his notepad and asked, "You had told Insp. Nemade that the deceased had warned you about the possible dire consequences in case you visited your father with Niranjan."

"Yes, I did make that statement and I still stand by it. But just because of that threat, I could not envisage her committing suicide. And I had made it clear to Nemade at the time," Ashvin explained.

"After this first phone she called you ten times. Out of these you did receive 3 calls and had a brief conversation. Didn't she suggest anything to that effect in those three calls?"

Madake very confidently glance at the Judge and brought an exaggerated expression of surprise while glancing at the audience.

Probably Ashvin too was prepared for this question. He replied steadfastly,

"No, she didn't suggest anything of the sort in those calls. She just kept repeating the same points.

Sorry Vakilsaheb, may I ask whether you are married or single? Or there are no arguments between you two? Are you naive about the way couples fight between them?"

The courtroom erupted into laughter, prompting the Judge to bang his gavel for silence. Mandake retorted sharply, "I am the one to ask questions, and you will have to stick to giving replies only. Understood?"

Ashvin apologized, but his demeanor contradicted his words.

Mandake questioned Ashvin sharply, "Between 3:37 and 3:49 PM, seven calls are registered, but you didn't bother to attend to a single one. Did you not feel that there could be some sort of emergency?"

"My father's age is 67. He is suffering from intestinal cancer for the last two years. He was very, very keen to meet his only grandson. Ketaki did not want me to take him there. 'The old man won't die so soon,' were her words. She uttered those words at least ten times…." There was a lump in Ashvin's throat. He could not speak further.

There was a pin-drop silence in the court. Ashvin continued with composure, "Hence I switched off the phone. I too I had lost my head."

Ad Avhad stood up and addressed the judge, seeking permission to pose a question regarding the matter. The judge looked towards Ad Mandake for confirmation, to which Mandake responded with a nonchalant gesture, indicating his compliance. With the approval of the court, Avhad proceeded to request Mr. Patil, the plaintiff, to take the witness stand.

Ad Avhad addressed the court, stating, "My client was questioned regarding his reluctance to respond to a series of calls from the deceased. It was implied that these calls may have been SOS signals intentionally ignored by my client, suggesting a preconceived strategy. I would like to pose a few questions to Mr. Patil, the plaintiff. I request him to take the witness stand."

As Patil approached the witness box, Ad Avhad began his line of questioning.

"Let us assume that the deceased was sending SOS signals and my client did not deem it necessary to respond. If she had been desperately trying to save her life, she should have contacted other people. Why didn't she try to contact you? Did she call you, and were you unable to answer her calls?"

"As a matter of fact, she called us twice, but we weren't at home. Our cell phone battery was dead, so we had left it behind."

Avhad feigned bewilderment and inquired, "Are you implying that you hadn't spoken to her on that day, yet you're accusing your son-in-law with such serious allegations?"

Mandake concluded the case with a succinct statement. By the time Avhad took charge, the judge and the audience had already formed a negative opinion about the deceased. Avhad wasted no time in capitalizing on this advantageous situation. While presenting the defendant's case, he asserted that the deceased was inherently extremist and had persistently attempted to alienate the defendant from his parents and his grandson from his ailing grandparents. Taking advantage of her husband's tolerant nature, she had manipulated the situation to her benefit. Furthermore, she maintained strained relations even with her own relatives.

Contrasting the negative portrayal of the deceased, Ashvin's image was painted as that of a tolerant husband, a dutiful and obedient son, and a caring father. He had never faltered in fulfilling his responsibilities as the sole son of his parents. Despite his demanding corporate role and responsibilities, he made concerted efforts to dedicate quality time to his son. Additionally, he maintained harmonious relations with his neighbors.

After establishing Ashvin's positive image, Avhad proceeded to raise a unique point altogether.

Avhad argued that in cases of suicide, if the individual desires to reverse their decision, they would typically send an SOS signal to those in close proximity, rather than contacting someone who is far away from the scene. Therefore, the likelihood of her calls being interpreted as SOS signals is minimal, he contended.

Furthermore, the fact that her cell phone was discovered in the far corner of the room suggests the possibility that she herself had thrown it when her calls were not attended by her husband and parents. This raises doubts about the circumstances surrounding her death.

Ultimately, Avhad made his appeal: "Considering all these facts, it can be concluded that Ashvin Shlke, my client, has nothing to do with the death of his ex-wife. I respectfully request His Highness to release him without any blemish."

The time allotted for the proceedings had expired, and the court adjourned without rendering a judgment in the case. The announcement of the verdict was scheduled to take place eight days later.

....

"Ashvin and Rahul arrived home in Pashan to find a beautiful rangoli adorning the entrance. Aai greeted them with a tray adorned with a holy lamp, betel nut, and auspicious rice grains. A group of neighboring ladies awaited their arrival, with Niranjan standing behind his aunt. The duo was received in a traditional manner by five ladies. Inside, Ashvin's father sat in the drawing room near his maternal uncles."

Recalling the countless challenges his parents had endured since his engagement to Ketaki, Ashvin felt a lump form in his throat. He knelt before his parents and lifted Niranjan with eyes glistening. Showering Niranjan with kisses, he whispered, 'my dear kid.' Ashvin's mother embraced them both warmly.

Aai consoled Ashvin, saying, "There, there! No more tears. Even in her departure from this world, she didn't spare you. But those sorrowful days are behind us now. Look at this innocent child and let's move forward." Despite her comforting words, tears streamed down Aai's cheeks.

It was a peculiar situation. Despite the recent tragic loss of their daughter-in-law, there was no sense of mourning within the Shelke family. Instead, relatives and well-wishers had gathered at their home to celebrate Ashvin's acquittal by the court. Ashvin found himself obliged to participate in the ceremony, although what he truly desired at that moment was solitude. He longed to be alone, with no one around him, not even Niranjan.

Erasing the memories of the past decade was not easy for Ashvin. However, what proved even more challenging was nurturing those memories. Leaving Niranjan to play with his cousins, Ashvin retreated to the solitude of his room. Closing the door behind him, he lay down on his bed.

His mind lingered on those painful memories against his wishes. He had met Ketaki at a wedding ceremony of his relatives, and it was love at first sight. Ketaki was 23 years old, and he was 26 at the time. Ashvin's parents did not approve of the relationship. They tried to prevent the wedding, disliking both Ketaki and her parents. Despite everyone's attempts to convince him of the impropriety of their marriage, Ashvin was overwhelmed by infatuation for Ketaki. He did not heed their advice and proceeded with the marriage. The parents had to yield to his desires. Now, he realized the immense price he had to pay for this mistake.

He used to feel excited even at the thought of her. He cherished every small gesture of hers, even her demands and arguments. It brought him joy to persuade her and fulfill her wishes. Every hug she gave him after an argument filled him with elation. She was passionate in bed when she wanted to be, using alluring tactics to entice him. Their quarrels and disagreements would dissolve in the intimacy of their shared moments. But today, he felt nothing but shame, far from any sense of longing.

Within a year, Ketaki's behavior underwent a drastic transformation. Subsequently, she made a deceptive suicide attempt and filed a police complaint against him and his elderly parents, dragging them to the police station without valid cause.

Aai succumbed to the stress, suffering her first heart attack. Baba's blood pressure soared. Their family became ostracized due to the humiliating situation she'd caused. Despite this, an inexplicable yearning for her presence gnawed at him. This overpowering longing was the root of this catastrophe.

'And yet... my vulnerable frame yearned for hers... It was this undeniable yearning that lay at the heart of this tragedy.' he concluded. He had believed that every family member ought to strive to comprehend one another and coexist harmoniously. However, what that 'harmony' truly entailed was Ketaki satisfying the cravings of his audacious body. Ultimately, Ashvin acquiesced to Ketaki's suggestion of establishing a separate household for them. However, this change failed to ameliorate the situation. Following Niranjan's birth, she wielded him as a tool to torment Ashvin and his parents. Recalling those agonizing memories was something Ashvin preferred to avoid.

He rose from the bed and reached for a thriller novel. He began reading it, yet not a single word registered in his mind. Unable to focus, he set the book aside, crossed his arms beneath his head, and stared blankly at the ceiling.

He remembered Nemade's stern gaze. "He had inquired repeatedly about the details of our last phone call. It was the most expected question, and I knew it well. Still, I stumbled over my words awkwardly. However, by the time Mandake reiterated the same question in court, I was ready for it. I had rehearsed every response meticulously in front of the mirror." He had endeavored to pinpoint the expressions that would be most persuasive to both the court and the prosecution. Additionally, he remembered the ripple of laughter that had swept through the courtroom when he had queried Mandake about his marital status...

He reminisced about the penultimate exchange with Ketaki, his heart quickening at the memory. "The old man isn't going to die so soon,' were her words that ignited something within him. Then, she had reached out again, uttering those chilling words, "You better come back... I have cut the veins on my wrist."

Ashvin refused to be swayed by such threats. He responded firmly, "You're not going to die. You're too careful not to harm yourself fatally. I won't be fooled by these tantrums."

"You can't do that. Have you forgotten your vows and your love for me? Don't you care about Niranjan?" she pleaded.

"Love? Whose love? Towards whom?" he retorted. "I'm not naive enough to love a cruel woman like you. That blue-eyed romantic Ashvin died long ago."

"There's a gush of blood from my wrist, please hurry up," Ketaki urged.

"I'm drinking insecticide. I feel dizzy... There's a burning sensation... Please come back," Ketaki declared between coughing fits, choked by the poison. Perhaps she was suffering, and yet...

In spite of that, Ashvin terminated the call and powered off the phone. He could have reached out to Vishwas, who was nearby. He could have intervened in time to save Ketaki. But Ashvin refrained from doing so.

He felt no remorse for her. There was not a trace of sympathy for Ketaki's suffering in his mind. He harbored no regret or remorse then, and even now...

The trail of thoughts and memories was abruptly interrupted by the sound of Niranjan's joyful laughter emanating from downstairs. Endearing comments from Baba and other relatives filled the air. It was a rare moment of happiness that the house hadn't experienced in quite some time.

Ashvin did not move from his bed and kept on sitting there. Aai came with a long needed cup of tea. Ashvin almost snatched the cup from Aai's hands and sipped tea like a thirsty man.

Aai was in tears. She hugged and caressed him. Ashvin's train of thoughts resumed as Aai left the room.

…..

I made a call to Vishwas after about an hour. My intention was to verify whether Ketaki had indeed carried out the heinous acts she had been threatening me with. Additionally, I wanted to ascertain if she had reached out to others for help.

But nobody answered the phone at Vishwas's house. The incessant ringing indicated that he wasn't reachable… or perhaps he was occupied trying to save her life. However, if that were the case, he would have promptly contacted me. Despite my cellphone being switched off, Vishwas had Baba's landline number. Then it struck me that both Vishwas and Shubha were supposed to attend a function that afternoon…

I was restless the entire evening, pacing anxiously in the drawing room. Half-expecting a call from Ketaki's father or brother, or perhaps from a hospital, but it never came. Perhaps it was just a threat, nothing more than her usual melodrama.

For quite some time, there had been no attempts to reach us on the landline. I switched on my cell phone and noticed a couple of missed calls from Ketaki. Still, nobody had tried to contact me directly. Despite feeling restless inside, I maintained my composure.

Niranjan and Baba were engrossed in watching the Pogo channel. Niranjan was explaining something to his grandfather, and Baba listened with evident pleasure. As time passed, it reached 5:45 PM. Approximately 20 minutes later, I left Baba's house with Niranjan.

On the way back, I found myself stuck in a traffic jam. Surprisingly, I wasn't annoyed. Instead of attempting to maneuver my way through the line of cars as I usually did, I remained patient.

It took some time to finally reach home. However, I hesitated to enter the house alone. I was half-expecting some sort of mishap, or perhaps she would start a fight the moment I walked in the door.

Perhaps Vishwas and Shubha hadn't returned home yet. It seemed plausible that Ketaki might be on the brink of death and could potentially be saved if discovered in time.

Taking advantage of Baba having given Niranjan a 20-rupee note for an ice cream cone, I bought one for him. The ice cream vendor seemed inclined to chat, and I wasn't in a rush to return home. Although it was challenging to maintain the conversation, it lasted a couple of minutes. Niranjan opted for a large cone, which bought us some extra time. He relished the ice cream, almost finishing it when I finally spotted Vishwas and Shubha near the community gate. Everything seemed to be perfectly timed.

The knock on the door shattered Ashvin's trail of memories. He attempted to discern his surroundings and recall his activities. To his relief, he realized he was in Pashan, at his Baba's house, in his own room.

"Who is it? Coming," he replied, making sure to observe his own expression as he passed by the mirror. Before opening the door, he paused in front of the mirror for a few seconds, striving to wear the appropriate expression on his face.

....

The Other Side of the Table

Manju stirred as the alarm pierced through the quiet of the morning. Blinking, she glanced at the clock to confirm it was indeed 7 o'clock. She reached for the pillow lying beside her, pressing it gently against her stomach as she lingered in bed for a few moments. Despite spending a couple of days in India, jet lag still lingered, stubbornly refusing to dissipate. However, she couldn't afford to indulge in more rest. The interview session loomed ahead at 9:30 a.m., a crucial engagement demanding her attention. Drawing from past experiences, she anticipated a flood of recent graduates from engineering colleges across the nation, each vying for coveted positions. The day would be consumed by interviews, each candidate scrutinized with precision as she sought to discern the best among them. Yet, beneath the surface, a weighty concern lingered. With each passing year, the quality of education seemed to falter, a trend that weighed heavily on her mind as she contemplated her return to the United States.

The coordinator responsible for the arrangements was scheduled to arrive at 8:30 a.m., tasked with escorting her to the Hotel Milton. Manju reflected with a sense of satisfaction on the exceptional treatment she received from her counterparts in India. "It's better here," she mused, pride coloring her thoughts. In India, individuals like her were accustomed to receiving royal treatment: a chauffeur-driven car at their disposal, a senior officer from the company attending to their every need, accompanied by subtle or overt compliments, and exotic meals served with care. In every possible way, she was pampered, a fact that never failed to leave her feeling indulged and appreciated.

Back in the United States, all the amenities were readily available, but such treatment to inflate one's ego was unheard of. Nowadays, even in India, top-notch five-star hotels provided efficient and hygienic service, with personalized attention given extra caution. Manju pondered these thoughts as she went through her morning routine. She meticulously styled her shoulder-length black hair, accentuated with brown streaks, and applied a light makeup to enhance her natural beauty. A gentle spritz of perfume completed her preparations. Adorning herself in her official western suit and coordinating costume jewelry, she couldn't help but admire her reflection in the mirror. There, she saw a reflection of her self-earned power, intelligence, efficiency, and innate beauty. Manju had always been meticulous about her appearance, believing it to be a reflection of her professionalism and self-respect.

When the intercom in her room buzzed just before 8 a.m., an unwilling crease appeared on Manju's forehead as she anticipated Mr. Sinha's arrival a few minutes later than the prearranged time. "Why is he here before time?" she muttered to herself as she picked up the phone.

The call was from the reception desk. "Sorry to disturb you, Ma'am, but there is somebody to see you, Ma'am," the receptionist informed her in a practiced, polite voice with a desi accent.

Manju disliked the use of the word "Ma'am," but begrudgingly acknowledged that it helped inflate her ego slightly. Her tone automatically shifted to an authoritative voice. "I don't want to entertain anyone right now. Please let me know when Mr. Sinha arrives. Is that clear?"

"Ya, Ma'am. But this lady here wants to have a word with you," replied the reception clerk.

"Okay, then give her the phone," Manju said grudgingly.

"Namaste, Mrs. Sandhya Nadkarni here. I teach at the Engineering college to the electrical students," the voice on the other end introduced herself.

Manju immediately recognized Mrs. Nadkarni from the Engineering college but pretended otherwise. "Okay, what brings you here? What is it that you wish to see me about?" she asked, feigning disinterest.

"I won't take your time. I wish to talk to you only for a couple of minutes. It is urgent. Please, will you see me?" Mrs. Nadkarni urged.

Manju hesitated before accepting the plea and said, "Okay. I cannot spare more than five minutes. I will come and meet you there in the lounge. You may wait there." She purposely did not try to conceal her American accent, subtly exerting pressure on the listener.

When Manju entered the lounge, she spotted an elderly, frail lady wearing glasses. The woman had clumsily attempted to dye her graying hair, likely in an effort to conceal her age. Manju would never have guessed that this was the same Prof. Mrs. Nadkarni. She was dressed in a starched, expensive cotton saree, much like before.

As Manju approached, the woman stood up from her seat and smiled uncertainly. She folded her hands in the conventional fashion to greet Manju. However, Manju ignored her greetings and extended her hand for a handshake. The action caused a slight sway in her earrings.

A pang of jealousy surged within Mrs. Nadkarni's heart as she observed Manju. 'Unlike us, these young girls are very lucky to get jobs, high posts, and money at such an early age,' she thought wistfully. 'They are blessed with the chance to go offshore to various countries. We had to work hard for years to achieve a senior position, let alone a high salary.' Yet, amidst her envy, there was a faint glimmer of hope. 'Today, there is a slight golden lining to this thought,' she reflected. 'My son, Shaunak, too, will achieve these things in the near future,' she mused, finding solace in the prospect of her son's success.

"Hi, nice to meet you. How can I help you?" asked Manju, extending a hand with a pleasant smile.

Mrs. Nadkarni was momentarily confused when approached by Manju, a stranger bearing a friendly smile. However, in a fraction of a second, recognition dawned upon her, and the color drained from her face. Memories flooded back of the past, when Manju looked quite different. Gone were the two plaits, replaced now by stylish bobbed hair. She had put on weight, which made her appear fairer, and her nose no longer seemed out of proportion thanks to her high cheeks. Yet, a light wound mark still adorned her left cheek, just below the eye, a faint reminder of times long past.

Mrs. Nadkarni felt a sudden urge to flee from the scene. She had come to meet the Vice President of 'Alien Cloud Computing Ltd,' Mrs. Ranade, unaware that Mrs. Ranade was none other than Manju Karkhanis, her former student. Had she known this beforehand, she would have never dared to seek her help in putting in a word for Shaunak. Now, she realized that doing so would not only fail to help her son but could potentially ruin his chances of selection.

"It seems you have not recognized me. I'm Manju Karkhanis, now Mrs. Ranade. I was your student, a 1997 pass-out," Manju informed her.

"Of course, I have recognized you, though I wasn't aware beforehand,' Mrs. Nadkarni responded.

"Eight years is not too short a period. You too have changed a lot," Manju remarked.

"I have heard a lot about you, but I did not know it was you. You are one of our best outgoing students," Mrs. Nadkarni continued.

Manju snapped in the middle of her sentence. "I can spare five minutes for you. Let us not waste time on preliminary introductions. What do you want me to do for you?"

Now Mrs. Nadkarni felt an overwhelming urge to vanish from the scene altogether. Yet, it was imperative to have this conversation with Manju. She began tentatively, "I'm feeling rather awkward to bring up this topic. I was told that the lady who was to interview the new candidates is an alumna of our college."

"How?" Manju inquired.

"Yesterday, some of our students were interviewed by you. They told my son about it," Mrs. Nadkarni explained.

Manju recalled mentioning her Alma mater to the candidates during the interviews. Though not particularly fond of her college, she had felt it necessary to share the information with candidates from the same institution.

"So?" Manju prompted.

"My son has also applied for the position. He hopes to get selected in 'Alien Cloud Computing Ltd.' It's his dream company," Mrs. Nadkarni admitted.

"Deserving candidates would be selected, and if he is in that category, then there won't..." Manju trailed off, leaving the sentence unfinished and shrugged her shoulders, as if to convey indifference.

Opening her shoulder bag, Mrs. Nadkarni took out a few papers and tried to convey, "His scores are very good, but he is aspiring for a US-based company, particularly 'Alien Cloud Computing Ltd.' As I said, he is passionate about it."

"Why so? Nowadays, many US-based companies come and recruit freshers for their company. Talking about this particular domain, there is ample scope with other players," Manju countered.

Mrs. Nadkarni persisted, pushing the papers into Manju's hands. "As you know, everyone has a dream, and it does not necessarily have any logic behind it. Shaunak is passionate about your company. Since last year, he has been aspiring to get entry. He says he was impressed by your site and started following it. He aspires to join the best company, and your company is at the top of his priority list."

Manju was reminded of her last year in college. She, too, was determined to enter L & T. There was no logic to it, yet she was passionate about her dream.

.....

Manju glanced briefly at Shaunak's CV and asked, "Why do you feel the need for a special recommendation for a candidate with such an impressive CV? He could secure a very good job anywhere. I don't necessarily mean in our company, but generally speaking, he wouldn't have any trouble."

"Five students from his class have received interview calls. In recent years, there has been a boom in the field of education, with many new engineering institutes emerging, making the competition very tough. He is eager to secure this job; otherwise, he would be frustrated," replied Mrs. Nadkarni.

"I understand your point, but I can't make any promises," Manju declared, ending further discussion.

For a few moments, Manju was lost in her past memories. Exactly eight years ago, her father had been in a similar position, urging this stubborn lady to come clean with the truth before the college authorities. However, she had refused to comply. Her refusal to reveal the truth behind the accident had not only ruined Manju's life but also Shrikant's, who had stood by her. Perhaps her expression gave away her deeper thoughts, prompting Mrs. Nadkarni to speak out, "Please spare one more minute. I urge you not to hold my past actions against my son. He is truly talented. The college had wronged you in the past, and I couldn't do anything to help you because I had my own compulsions."

"Achcha! Are you implying that I shouldn't be unjust to Shaunak?" Manju clarified.

"Believe me, I didn't know that you would be the one interviewing him. Shaunak insisted that I meet you, knowing you're an alumna of our college," Mrs. Nadkarni explained.

"But it seems that has backfired, hasn't it?" Manju remarked.

Mrs. Nadkarni helplessly wiped sweat from her forehead and requested Manju to forget about the past.

"Even my Dad was urging you to come clean, and you expect me to forget that too?" Manju's voice lost its professional tone and became harsh with rage. Her expression shifted from normal to angry in an instant.

She noticed Mr. Sinha approaching their direction, prompting her to quickly switch back to a cordial expression. Leaving Mrs. Nadkarni bewildered and alone, Manju stepped in his direction. Mrs. Nadkarni could only watch helplessly as their figures receded.

Mrs. Nadkarni had to admit that she had wronged not only Manju but also her other prized student, Shrikant, for siding firmly with Manju and fighting for her.

It was the final year of that batch. Though Mrs Nadkarni was not directly connected with the sad incident, as the head of the department, she was required to face the higher authorities and provide explanations. Maintenance of the workshop machinery was never within the purview of the H O D's responsibility. Nobody gives you any credit until things run smoothly, but the moment anything goes wrong, you are held responsible. Anything could have happened, and the media would have brought it to the public platform. She would have to face the music.

Around 2:30 p.m., Mrs. Nadkarni had just returned to the staff room after finishing two consecutive lectures. She was about to order a cup of steaming coffee when panicked Balu rushed to her with news of a tragic accident in her lab. There had been a serious accident during the practical session of the fourth-year students' batch. A small part of the DC current checking machine had slipped and hit a student, as Balu informed her.

Mrs. Nadkarni found herself torn between whether or not to go to the accident spot. She weighed the potential consequences of witnessing or avoiding the site visit. Eventually, she decided to go, as it was clear she was nowhere near the workshop when the mishap occurred.

The students had gathered in small groups, talking in hushed voices. Mrs. Nadkarni could see Manju lying prostrate in a pool of blood, streaks of fresh blood dripping from her left cheek. Her clothes were stained with blood, and a couple of girls were trying to support and console her. Shrikant was sitting nearby, asking whether she was hurt anywhere other than what was easily traceable. Somebody offered her a glass of water, and a few others tried to administer first aid. The lab assistant was himself confused but trying to manage the terrified students. This had never happened before.

Somebody brought a rickshaw to the back door of the lab, and Manju's friends helped her into it, holding her on both sides. It would have been appropriate for Mrs. Nadkarni to accompany Manju, yet she decided that it was more important to investigate the cause of the incident and determine the person responsible for it. As the H O D, she conveniently prioritized this as her first responsibility, leaving the other responsibility with the students.

The lab assistant and the technician were palpably disturbed. It was their joint responsibility to maintain the equipment, meticulously following scheduled check-ups and oiling. They both swore that there was no oversight in this respect. They claimed that the concerned machine was routinely checked by them, and they had not detected any flaws in it. However, they could not provide any explanation for why the accident happened, pleading their inability to do so.

The technician made Balu vow for it, stating that he was supposed to clean the floor after the technician and lab assistant had finished their work.

"Balu, in turn, tried to pass the parcel to the technician, saying, 'Yes, both of them were working on the machine, that I can vouch for. But I don't know what or how they did it.'" Balu added.

The lab assistant then stepped forward to clarify the matter, telling Mrs. Nadkarni, "Mam, I am not supposed to check each and every equipment before every use. Yet, I usually do it for the sake of students' safety. Even today, I had examined it, and everything was in place. Probably this girl's scarf or stole might have entangled in the machine, loosening the bolt. These girls always wear loose and fashionable clothes with stoles while experimenting in the lab. That's why such accidents occur," he concluded.

Thus, the blame game started, with each one passing the parcel to the other person.

It was indeed very difficult to ascertain the true culprit in such a situation. In that case, the Principal would have held Mrs. Nadkarni responsible. Manju's parents would have gone to the press or even taken legal action, Mr. Nadkarni surmised.

Like a cat always making sure to fall on all fours, it was her motto to safeguard herself every time she found herself in a tricky situation. She started planning in that direction, making all the present students wait in the lab. She then made a detailed report of the incident, claiming that the part of the said machine was loosened by the stole worn by Manju Karkhanis. Thus, the college staff was not to be held responsible for the accident, she firmly declared in that report. Only fifteen students were still present, and they were asked to sign the declaration.

Two girls claimed that they could not see Manju from where they were standing and hence they could not sign. Nishad, the Magazine secretary, argued that Manju was nowhere near the machine when the accident took place, and there was no possibility of her stole entangling in the machine. He claimed that even Shrikant would vouch for that because he too was next to Manju at that time. He flatly refused to sign the document.

Now Mrs. Nadkarni was nonplussed. If any of the students had given a statement opposing the declaration, it would have caused turbulence. If Nishad and Shrikant had convinced their classmates about it, the others too would have refused to comply with it. They had a nuisance value, she mused.

She felt like a trapped animal. Her promotion was due shortly. Although she had been chosen as the temporary head of the department, it had not been endorsed by the concerned authorities. Her fate was in the hands of the principal's kitchen cabinet, where her guide held sway. It was up to him whether or not to declare her doctoral work sufficient to grant her the degree. In such a situation, this sudden development would have been a significant hurdle for her.

The only way out seemed to be the fact that granting of internal assessment marks depended solely on the H O D and the concerned examiner. The whole career of the students depended on those crucial internal marks. They would need recommendations and transcripts depending upon their further decisions.

"I want no arguments; everybody needs to comply with my order. Otherwise, disciplinary action will be taken against those not complying with it. I don't want any discussion on this point. Is that understood?" she almost threatened them.

Most of the students surrendered before the threat and signed it, after which even Nishad could not stand by his own vow. Yet he murmured, "I will not sign this paper before consulting Manju," and left the lab.

Mrs. Nadkarni was annoyed with Nishad, as he seemed to threaten her ingeniously crafted plan. It was only because of Manju's and Shrikant's absence that she had mustered the courage to go ahead with her plan. On the third day, Shrikant came to know about the things being planned against Manju in their absence. He met Mrs. Nadkarni and explained, "I think you have been misinformed. I read your report on the accident; it was not due to Manju's stole entangling the machine that triggered the accident. Manju was five feet away from the machine when the accident took place. She had worn a cotton stole and had securely tied it at the back. I have written down the course of events for you. All the students of our batch would vouch for it."

Mrs. Nadkarni could not control her anger. She never wanted this discussion to happen in the presence of her colleagues in the staff room. She asked Shrikant to keep those papers on her desk and leave the staff room. Possibly she could not think of a better reason to put an end to the discussion.

In the same evening, she summoned a few students including Nishad and Shrikant and coolly informed them, "I have no misgivings about the sad event. I have talked to the lab assistant and the technician only after which I drafted the report. Look for yourself, everybody from your class has signed it."

Both of them did not budge. They were prepared to go to the principal if need arose. Except for Shrikant, everyone complied with her order without resistance. During all these days, it did not occur to her that she should have gone to see Manju in the hospital or at home and made sure she was out of danger. All were scared to observe Manju's broken front teeth, swollen face, and almost closed left eye. Nobody knew whether she would be able to see with that eye.

After a week, Manju's father came to the college to meet Mrs. Nadkarni, with Shrikant accompanying him. Mrs. Nadkarni wrongly inferred that he was there to lodge a complaint against her. Hence, she was in an aggressive stance to defend herself.

"It was an accident. Manju's stole got entangled in the machine, and hence this accident took place. College authorities are in no way responsible for that. There is no chance of you getting compensated by the college," she asserted.

Manju's father was aggrieved to watch this lady struggling to save her skin. He interjected, "We do not expect compensation from the college. I would willingly bear all the expenses. I have come here with a request to rearrange Manju's oral exams. You know her academic record. She has stood first in all the semesters. She is not in a position to open her eyes and read for herself. I urge you to please postpone her orals on medical grounds. "She is my daughter, and I would do anything to get her cured," Manju's father emphasized, his concern and determination evident in his voice.

Mrs. Nadkarni was somewhat pacified after that. She asked him, "Then why are you here?"

"There's not a grain of truth in the report you have meticulously made. You know it, and I too am aware of it. Had you or anyone on behalf of the institute bothered to come and visit her, you would have known what she and her family were undergoing. It is not possible for her to study for the exam, and hence this request."

"I appreciate your concern. But we cannot interfere in the schedule laid down by the University," she declared without qualms.

Dad continued to pester that shameless lady with his requests, after which she promised to give it a try.

After a couple of meetings Mrs Nadkarni's plea was somehow accepted, and Manju's exam was rearranged after a couple of days. Shrikant was regarded as a traitor and duly punished. He had answered all the tricky questions in his usual fashion. She gave him marks barely enough to pass, while the external examiner had given him a good remark and more marks.

Mrs. Nadkarni had to admit that at that time both Shrikant and Manju were as novice as Shaunak was now. Yet she did not give them the advantage of their age. She had no ill feeling for Manju; all she wished was to save her own skin at any cost.

The past incident would likely become a hurdle in the way of Shaunak, she mused sadly. Power, position, and affluence had transformed Manju completely, she concluded.

………

After talking to Mrs Nadkarni, Manju went for the interview session and she still was preoccupied with the lingering past memories. The thought of calling Shrikant to share the unexpected encounter with Mrs. Nadkarni brought a smile to her face.

The students were coming with lot of apprehension and replying to the questions posed by her according to their ability. Shaunak entered the room just before the lunch break. It was clear from his body language that he was stressed. Many of the earlier candidates had been palpably street smart. Shaunak's appearance was comparatively sober and simple. His basic concepts were very clear and hence while replying he looked to be confident. He took his own time to think over the question before replying. His communication skill was much superior to that of students from English medium schools run by Marathi folk. Had she been not informed about his parent she would not have hesitated in selecting him, Manju admitted to herself. Some more candidates were scheduled for the next day, after which she would have to declare the list of selected ones.

In the evening, while returning to the hotel, she again thought about calling Shrikant. Shrikant had posted about his upcoming Europe tour on Facebook the previous week. She would have to take into account the time difference in Europe, which would be approximately five hours behind Indian standard time, she calculated. Sinha had already fixed a dinner with her counterparts from India. She was supposed to reach there by eight PM. As soon as she reached the venue, she declared that she would not be able to linger for more than an hour.

Ultimately, she managed to contact Shrikant at half past ten. Shrikant replied immediately.

Manju wasted no time in the preliminaries and declared, "Hi Shrikant. Today, an interesting incident happened. Hence this call."

"A pleasant surprise. How come you could find time at this hour? No office today?" he reciprocated.

"I am not in the office. I am in India for the interviews. A very funny thing happened, and I cannot wait to tell you about it."

"Shoot, I'm listening."

"Guess who had come for the interview?"

"You are still the same old girl with the habit of making people guess about small things. How would I be able to guess? Go ahead and tell me."

"Shaunak Nadkarni, Nadkarni Mam's son."

Shrikant whistled from the other end.

"Listen to what happened before it. Mam had come to put in a word for her son! What do you have to say?"

"Of all persons, she approached you? How could she do that?"

"Now I am Mrs Ranade and she had no clue to my real personality. When she looked at me, she lost her courage, and the color drained from her face. Inside, I was tickled to death."

"You must have given her a hard time."

"How could I not take advantage of the situation?"

Then Manju narrated the whole thing about how their alumna had come for the interview the earlier day and spreading the news of her belonging to the same college. Mrs. Nadkarni's son insisted that she meet Manju for her recommendation.

"Ayla! She must have regretted her action! Whatever little hope she had nurtured might have ebbed after it."

"You must have seen her face, Shrikant."

"I would have rather loved to watch your arrogant face while dealing with her!"

"I was boiling with mirth inside. She admitted the blunder she had committed eight years back. She also asked me not to hold it against her son as a revenge. I reminded her how my Dad was urging her at the time and asked her whether she expected me to forget that too!... She was nonplussed."

That took them on a journey through the memory lane about the incident and those bygone days. Afterward, Shrikant asked her a pertinent question, "What is your impression about this Shaunak? Irrespective of his parent, how did you find him as a candidate?"

"He is good... but not very smart. He was visibly scared and under stress."

"Isn't it obvious? He must have thought that his Mom's recommendation would turn into a disqualification. Have you selected him or rejected him?"

"That stage has not yet arrived. He is on hold. I am in two minds. What is your opinion?"

"I have not interviewed him. But one thing is certain. You should not decide on what Mam had done to you all those years back. Had you not known about his connection to Mrs. Nadkarni, what would you have done?"

"I don't know. Probably, I would have selected him. His academic performance is remarkable without any blemishes, with distinction in all the semesters."

"We both have experienced how one at the receiving end feels when wrongly accused. I don't think you would like any other student experiencing it, do you? Luckily for us, that incident could not do us any harm in our careers. In spite of everything, we could go ahead. Now there are many avenues open before this new generation, but the competition has also increased. The problems they are facing now are more complicated than at our times... So..."

"Does it mean that I should go ahead and select him on pure merit? Your opinion is of crucial importance to me. Mam had wronged both of us. You were unnecessarily punished just because you stood steadfast with me. I would feel like betraying you and our friendship and your sacrifice..."

"You need not bring our friendship into these official matters, I urge. You cannot disqualify a deserving candidate out of personal grievances. I would never feel you did justice to our friendship by it. Would you feel so?"

"Won't you be offended if I select him? I have an opportunity to take revenge and yet I am not taking advantage of it. Would you be hurt because of my action?"

"Mam was a coward. She did it just to save her skin and it was not forgivable. I would never justify it, but we can understand her predicament; many issues were at stake... Now there is nothing for you to stake out. You won't be affected in either way, even if you reject or select him."

"I won't be benefited in either case. Of course, except for the satisfaction of doing justice to you and me. Now let me ask you bluntly, what would you have done if placed in my position?"

For a few minutes, there was complete silence on the other end. Manju had to check the internet connectivity; she found it to be in place.

"Tell me, what would you have done?" she asked.

"Probably I would have done what you are now doing. I would have been in a fix, whether or not to forgive and forget the past and select the candidate without talking to you. I would have called you and consulted about your opinion. At least I would have discussed the issue with you."

"I feel much better now. I am on the right track, I guess. Now I would be able to decide the action with an open mind. Thanks."

"Who is to decide right or wrong? We both are thinking on the same lines; that much we can say. We feel like following certain values and norms even when placed on the other side of the table. Let us decide not to be corrupted even in the future."

"You are perfectly right. Good night and thanks for everything, my friend."

"Same to you." Shrikant concluded the discussion with inner satisfaction for both concerned.

....

The Promise

During my 25 years of medical practice, I encountered numerous challenging cases. There were moments when I felt overwhelmed, grappling with situations slipping out of my control. However, the ordeal Mrs. Mhatre plunged me into is etched in my memory like no other. Perhaps it's because I was still a novice at the time, having recently commenced my practice. The sheer terror of the situation lingers, considering the potential consequences: not only could it have jeopardized my license but also my reputation, despite my innocence in the matter. The truth is, I was utterly shaken. If it hadn't been for Daddy standing steadfastly behind me like a rock, I might have collapsed under the weight of it all.

The era of super specialization had just begun. My belief was that after completing my M S in general surgery, instead of immediately starting to practice at our own hospital, it would be wiser to spend a few months practicing at a general hospital to gain experience with a variety of cases. Dad did not object to this plan. At that time, the incidence of kidney problems was on the rise in the country. Dad was not too old to manage our hospital for another couple of years. Our hospital had only 12 beds, and our intention was to expand it before I joined there.

After completing three terms at Jaslok Hospital, I resigned from my position and joined our hospital as a nephrologist. Although patients naturally preferred well-equipped, well-known hospitals like Nanavati, Hinduja, and Jaslok, there was always a shortage of available beds. People were afraid of the hefty bills patients were known to incur upon discharge. Urban areas in Maharashtra rarely had fully equipped hospitals for such complex surgeries, so there was a constant influx of patients from those regions to Mumbai. The most significant advantage I gained from my job at Jaslok was visibility among patients. Therefore, many patients did not feel the need to insist on Jaslok and were willing to be admitted to our hospital if I was to treat them. Often, people preferred our hospital for post-surgery care and follow-up sessions. They did not see the need to go to these hospitals for dialysis. Of course, our hospital could not boast of having all the state-of-the-art equipment for intricate procedures, but in such cases, patients had the option to visit these hospitals as outpatients.

During this time, Mr Mhatre's case came to my attention. Dr. Bapat, my old batch mate who settled in the Kokan region, had referred his case to me. He suspected a malfunctioning kidney in Mr. Mhatre and sent him to see me. The Mhatres were hoping for a misdiagnosis, but I knew there was little chance that Bapat would make such a gross mistake in diagnosis. Mr. Mhatre's symptoms also suggested kidney malfunction. There were many other complications in his case: he was diabetic, had a long history of hypertension, and his respiratory tract was severely affected by his long-standing habit of smoking, particularly bidis—the strongest indigenous form of cigarettes. Therefore, treatments intended for one ailment often interfered with the treatment of another. Many times, we doctors also hope for an erroneous diagnosis for the sake of helpless patients, but it rarely happens.

Mrs. Mhatre and their young son had accompanied him. Their hopes solely depended on my opinion. Usually, patients in such critical situations find themselves utterly helpless, and the Mhatres were no exception. Mrs. Mhatre had gathered all the courage she could muster. On one hand, she was trying to understand the patient's condition, and on the other, she was attempting to support her husband emotionally. Despite her efforts, she seemed to be on the verge of collapse. She was of my mother's age and had the same temperament, which naturally made me very concerned about her.

I was in a dilemma. It was a herculean task not to raise their hopes and, at the same time, make them strong enough to face the eventuality. As a rule, no doctor should get emotionally involved with their patients. I was fully aware of this rule, and yet I found it challenging to adhere to it. The Mhatres had approached the doctor in an advanced stage of the disease, and the patient's age was not in his favor—he was over seventy. If they had come to me a little earlier, it might have made some difference. His body had effectively concealed its issues by not showing any outward impact of the inner ailment. And whatever symptoms were visible were attributed by the Mhatres to known ailments like hypertension and diabetes. When the body could no longer hide the symptoms and started swelling, they had approached Dr. Bapat. He wasted no time in getting various tests done and directed them to me.

After conducting all the necessary tests, my diagnosis proved to be correct. The kidneys had ceased to function under the pressure of age-old diabetes. To exacerbate matters, it was discovered that the patient was born with only one kidney, and the remaining one had started to fail due to overwork. On the third day, while the clinical tests were still incomplete, the patient slipped into a coma. We had to immediately transfer him to Jaslok Hospital. After a week, some symptomatic relief was observed, and I brought him back to our hospital. During those days, I treated him based solely on the current symptoms. That was all I could do.

The Mhatres were staying with their close relatives in the Dadar area, conveniently located near our hospital. Given the patient's condition, it was imperative to administer frequent rounds of dialysis, and I advised Atul, the patient's son, clearly about this. While discussing the treatment plan, I also emphasized the potential costs involved, although I was unaware of their financial situation. Such expenses, including lodging and boarding for close relatives in a big city like Mumbai, can often be unmanageable for middle-class families. Moreover, it would have been challenging to sustain this arrangement indefinitely.

It was highly likely that the patient would have needed ongoing dialysis treatment. He seemed to struggle with the procedure, his tolerance diminishing rapidly each passing day. Mrs. Mhatre was frequently by his side, speaking softly in an attempt to comfort him. Unfortunately, I couldn't witness these moments firsthand.

Every time she saw me, Mrs. Mhatre would ask, "Isn't he better today? He looks better than yesterday. Won't he come out of it soon?"

I dared not tell her the truth. It becomes increasingly difficult for the doctor if the patient looks at you as if you are next to God and are sure to have a remedy for every ailment. I was put in that tricky situation. Kidney transplant surgeries were not very common in those days. Nobody could guarantee success in those surgeries. There used to be ample post-surgery complications, and despite a successful surgery, the patient used to be susceptible to some kind of infection, and hence the survival rate was meager. I could sense the fear of possibility of death in Mrs. Mhatre's timid eyes. The one thing which we doctors cannot do is give up and advise the patients to stop the efforts. We always try to fight till the last moment.

Why do we do that? Do we wish to try and test our own skill, capability and dexterity? Nowadays, I feel that sometimes we unnecessarily try to play God. But back then, I did not think on those lines. Had they gone ahead and paid for the exorbitant expenditure for almost a hopeless case, all I could have done for them was to forgo my fees.

Yet I made up my mind and called both the mother and the son to explain the facts to them. Even today, I vividly remember that scene. Atul sat in front of me, staring hard. He might have been younger than me by a couple of years. Due to my profession, I was exposed to human life and death, but such was not the case with him. He might have been settled in his profession, but was nowhere near the truth regarding human life and death. His mother was palpably restless, uneasily playing with her handkerchief.

I cleared my throat and began, "I am going to explain and share everything with you. You must already be aware of the earlier complications due to co-existing ailments and about the seriousness of the patient's condition. All the systems in the human body are interlinked and interrelated. Hence, it is much more difficult for a patient with preexisting ailments to fight a new ailment than a person in perfectly healthy condition."

"Yes, I know, but what's wrong with him at the moment? What treatment is necessary in this condition?" Atul asked, sounding like an innocent child.

I showed them the chart of the human body systems, pointing out the location and function of the kidneys. I also explained that the patient had been lacking one kidney since birth and the other had stopped working. Mrs. Mhatre listened attentively.

"Does it mean that he cannot be cured at all?" she asked, her face draining of color. She looked at me intently, awaiting a reply.

"There is a treatment, but it won't be able to cure him," I explained. "He will be temporarily relieved of the symptoms, but they will keep reappearing intermittently. We will have to give the same treatment again and again. This will go on indefinitely."

Both of them remained quiet for a few minutes.

Without explicitly mentioning the word 'death,' I conveyed to them in gentle words that at most, we could only postpone the inevitable. It would have been easier for me to be straightforward if Mrs. Mhatre wasn't present. However, I couldn't ask her to leave the room as it might have been misconstrued. But she seemed to read my mind and got up suddenly.

"I will be with my husband. Will you please discuss things with my son alone?" she asked.

I nodded as she left the room. Later, I could be more candid with Atul. I discussed the seriousness of the ailment, the potential pain and discomfort from the available treatments, and the inevitable expenditure. I left the decision in their hands, which gave me some relief. Atul promised to consult his parents and let me know their decision. I advised him to take as much time as necessary. Until then, our hospital would provide the necessary care, I assured him.

Since then, Mrs. Mhatre stopped asking me about the patient's condition, which somewhat relieved me. Whenever I entered their room, I would see Mrs. Mhatre reading religious scriptures or chanting with beads by the patient's bedside, wearing a somber expression. I couldn't help but feel empathy for her. Our conversation had reached its conclusion. Atul had left a message for me, informing me that he had gone to their place for a couple of days.

By then, Dad had noticed that I was becoming increasingly disturbed by this case. He tried to console me with words of wisdom and personally visited the patient as well. He took it upon himself to ensure Mrs. Mhatre's comfort, spending time talking to her. Suddenly, the patient's condition worsened just after Atul left for Konkan. He struggled to breathe properly, and we arranged for an oxygen cylinder near his bed, increasing the dose to alleviate his symptoms. Thankfully, he showed some improvement the next day. We questioned why Atul had left during such a critical emergency, only to learn that he had gone to arrange finances. It was evident that Atul had fully briefed Mrs. Mhatre about the patient's condition before leaving.

It was a shock when the patient's condition suddenly deteriorated despite all the care taken and the improvement observed the previous day. Unfortunately, I wasn't at the hospital when this happened. I had scheduled operations for two patients at Jaslok and three at K. E. M. before leaving. Everything seemed fine when I checked before departing. However, around half past four in the early evening, I received an urgent message from Sister Kamble. At the time, I was discussing a case with Dr. Kotwal. Sister Kamble's voice sounded panicked, urging me to come quickly without providing any specific details.

When I arrived at the hospital, Sister Kamble was waiting for me at the reception.

"Doctor, we need to hurry to room number four," she declared upon seeing me, deviating from our usual decorum.

We didn't exchange a word until we reached the first floor. Sister opened the door, her fingers trembling as she slid back the door hasp. Sweat broke out on my forehead as I took in the scene. The oxygen mask had been forcefully removed, and the needle delivering saline had been taken out of the wrist. His head was tilted to the left, and his lips were covered with foam. I immediately grasped the severity of the situation. The second bed and Mrs Mhatre's chair were both vacant.

There was no need to check his pulse, but I did so nonetheless.

"Does Mrs. Mhatre know about this? Where is she?" I inquired.

"She's nowhere to be found," the Sister replied.

Though I felt somewhat relieved by her absence, I asked the Sister in a terse voice, "How could this happen while you were on duty?"

"At three, I administered an injection, and he was fine then. Mrs. Mhatre was with him in this chair," the scared Sister replied timidly.

I lost my cool. Sister Kamble had worked with us for the last two decades. Until that moment, there had been no reason to doubt her efficiency, expertise, and sincerity. But there was no one else to shout at other than her and release my tension.

"Did I ask you about your whereabouts at three pm? Where were you, and what were you doing when this catastrophe occurred? You are responsible for the patients in my absence. Do you expect me to be here twenty-four hours inspecting things?" I shouted.

"I was at the counter, Sir. Everything was in place when I made a couple of rounds in the ward," she replied, tears flowing from her eyes.

"How come this bed is vacant? Where is the other patient?" I asked.

"He was shifted to room number two, where he had requested. I moved him at two o'clock. Mrs. Mhatre was relaxing in her chair at the time," she explained giving unessential and irrelevant details.

"Where could the senior Sir be? Call him immediately," I ordered.

"Sir, he is being informed. He has left Lonavala before two o'clock and should be back any time," she informed.

"Leave a message for him to hurry to the hospital as soon as he can," I instructed.

"Yes, Sir."

"Who else knows about this incident?"

"No one," she replied.

I could imagine the devastating chain of events that would unfold. A police case would be inevitable, tarnishing our hospital's reputation. It would lead to a scandal, and my career would be ruined. All my dreams would be shattered because of this oversight.

"Now, close the door and put up a 'Do not disturb' sign. Bring Mrs. Mhatre to my office as soon as she returns... Sister, do you realize the serious implications of this incident? Not only my and Dad's reputations are at stake, but also your job and career. So…"

I was very blunt and harsh with the sister. Perhaps to me, that was the only way to ensure her silence. She would have kept it a secret to protect herself.

I sat in my office, my head in my hands, waiting for Dad to return. I don't know how long I stayed like that. Suddenly, there was a knock on the door. It could be Dad, I thought. The door opened, and I looked up to see the ward boy entering with a tray of coffee. Sister had sent two cups. Dad came in after the ward boy left, and seeing me in that state, he collapsed into the chair opposite me. I wanted to tell him everything, but Dad insisted that I have some coffee first.

I narrated every detail to Dad, and surprisingly, he listened patiently without interrupting with questions to me.

"Where is Mrs. Mhatre?" he asked.

"She is not in the hospital. It seems that every day she goes somewhere during this time," I replied.

Dad called Sister Kamble. After speaking with her, Dad concluded that no one had seen Mrs. Mhatre after three fifteen. Sister had the phone number of the Mhatre's relatives. Sister was about to call that number when there was a knock on the door. Mrs. Mhatre and a young man entered the room.

Mrs. Mhatre had lost color in her face. She couldn't stand still or speak coherently. Her young companion looked bewildered and angry. Dad made them sit and talk.

"My name is Unmesh Walawalkar. I have accompanied this lady," he said, staring at Mrs. Mhatre and urging her to speak. However, she remained silent.

"We were trying to contact you. Mr. Mhatre's condition worsened, and we couldn't place her anywhere," Dad informed them cautiously.

"I know what went wrong with the patient. She is also aware of it. She has brought all of us into jeopardy by her silly, impulsive action. My father is not at home, and Mom panicked after hearing her story. In the end, I had to come with her," Unmesh clarified in his own way. This left us with more doubts.

Gradually, Dad and I could guess what might have happened. The woman whom I considered as my own Mom was responsible for this deed? I had considered her to be a simple, righteous and God-fearing individual. Was it an oversight or a well planned, deliberate action? Why was she inclined to do it? All these thoughts came to my mind in a fraction of a second.

Now, Dad took hold of the situation and said, "She has brought our lives also in danger. Please tell us what and how things happened." Dad asked her in a firm but soft voice.

"I made a blunder. But believe me, it did not occur to me that I am jeopardizing others' lives by my spontaneous action. My husband had made me promise that I will abide by his wish," Mrs. Mhatre whispered in a barely audible voice visibly trembling in the chair.

"What are you talking about? What promise?" asked Dad.

"Long back, both of us had promised each other that in case any one of us is diagnosed with an incurable disease, the other will help end his or her life. He was reminding me of that promise and insisting that I fulfill it," she looked at me and continued, "The other day, the doctor gave me an idea about his ailment and I was convinced that it is the beginning of an end. But my husband had guessed it long back."

She started sobbing. But I had no empathy for her. All I thought about was the possibility of her not lodging a police complaint and the resultant catastrophe.

My worst fear was misplaced. Patients' relatives are often inclined to lodge police complaints. I feared how to dissuade her from lodging a complaint. However, in this case, that possibility was ruled out. Mrs. Mhatre was declaring that she herself had removed the support system. We, our hospital, and Sister Kamble were out of the shadow of doubt and the resulting scandal. I was devoid of earlier stress. Despite that, I was ashamed of my own selfish thoughts. I couldn't understand how I could be so insensitive and callous. I had absolutely no idea about Dad's inner thoughts. He seemed reasonable and poised.

He started talking in an empathetic voice, "Look here Mrs Mhatre, I can understand your feelings... Let me tell you one thing, however pure the intentions behind the action, it's a legal offense to put an end to anybody's life. Even your son would hold us responsible for his death and accuse us of negligence. What are we to do then?" At the end of the sentence Dad's voice lost its empathetic hint and turned angry.

Unmesh chose this moment to intervene.

"Since these people are staying at our home, we are unnecessarily connected with this issue. Tomorrow there would be exaggerated stories in the newspaper. I always advise my parents not to get involved with their remote relatives. But they never pay attention. When it comes to people from their native place, they reach out with helping hands. The times have changed. Nobody should get involved in other people's personal problems." Unmesh vented his suppressed anger further expressing his frustration. He inadvertently muttered abusive words under his breath.

It was understandable that he would be frustrated. Ordinary people aren't often confronted with such calamitous situations.

It seemed like everyone was focused on protecting themselves. However, the person most at risk was unaware of the potential consequences and legal implications. Despite grappling with the grief of losing her beloved husband, she passionately explained the rationale behind her actions. Yet, there was a sense of remorse evident in her haunted eyes.

"Doctor, I won't allow that to happen, I assure you. All of you have helped us in times of difficulty, and I am indebted to you for it. I will talk to Atul," she said.

"You are not in a proper frame of mind. You are not aware of the possible implications of your actions, I'm afraid. Are you confident that even your son will forgive you for your action?" asked Dad.

Even at that moment, I was amazed at the cool-headed stance with which Dad was handling the situation. It would have been inconvenient for us if Mrs. Mhatre had confided in Atul. He might have seen it as his duty as a son to seek justice for his late father. It would have been difficult to dissuade him from taking such action. All we needed was the patient's death certificate. Once that was obtained and the body cremated, there would be no grounds to accuse us of negligence. By that time, all evidence would have been destroyed.

Mrs. Mhatre seemed on the verge of saying something but held back, perhaps not having fully considered her son's potential reaction in the given situation. She physically collapsed in front of us, and Sister Kamble quickly moved to support her. Unmesh and I assisted Sister Kamble in placing her on the examination table. Dad retrieved a syringe and injection bulb, and Sister Kamble administered it to Mrs. Mhatre. Within a couple of minutes, she began to recover. It felt inhumane to continue discussing matters further at that moment. Yet, we were left with no choice but to make immediate decisions.

It was difficult not to reflect on the fact that each of us in that room was equally in need of rescue, and that realization offered a convenient escape for us all. Mrs. Mhatre's identity as a loyal, devout, and caring wife appeared to lose significance, even to her, when confronted with the prospect of her son abandoning her. The fervor of her love had waned.

It became much easier to persuade Mrs. Mhatre to keep things unsaid. Dad offered her solace with his words of wisdom. "It wouldn't be in your best interest to make this public. Consider this: Mr. Mhatre's condition was critical from the beginning. Even if you hadn't removed the support system, he was destined to pass away in a couple of days. Let's all agree that what happened was not a result of your actions; it was a natural death. There's no need for anyone else to know the truth, and the chance of the news leaking is minimal. You can decide later whether to confide in Atul or not. The choice is yours."

Everybody was amenable to this suggestion.

Dad didn't loosen his grip on the situation. That day, I learned the value of maturity that comes with age and experience.

Mrs. Mhatre willingly accepted the proposal, which proved to be less troublesome for all parties involved. Atul, who was en route to Mumbai, was duly informed, and everything unfolded smoothly according to our plans.

Throughout the rituals, Mrs. Mhatre remained silent. Dad didn't forget to advise Atul to consider taking her to a psychologist if needed. Given the circumstances, there wasn't much else we could do. We never crossed paths with the Mhatres again. Whether Mrs. Mhatre confided in her son remains unknown. Every time I think of Mrs. Mhatre, I'm reminded of the depth of her emotions and the narrow-mindedness of my own selfish thoughts.

....

The Religion

Huge branches of tall, sturdy trees lined the narrow mud road, swaying with the wind. Many tiny flower-laden shrubs adorned the sides of the road, and among them, green lush grass blades were swinging. The wind hissed, mingling with the sound of running water, while the ringing of bells from the Shiv temple echoed in the air. We ran down the slope of the road, our uncontrollable feet picking up speed, laughter bubbling from our lips.

As we entered the open space, the solid stone door of the temple intermittently came into view, although the sculptures on it could not be seen from this distance. We loved to visit the inside of this temple and chant the mantra "Om Namah Shivaya" when it resonated. We often competed with each other, elongating the 'Om'. I was about to enter the temple when somebody placed his firm and strong palm on my shoulder, as if to stop me from entering. I struggled to release myself from the firm grip without success. Observing the big red stone on the ring, I realized it must be none other than Ahmad.

'None else could have such a strong and demanding grip. It can't be promising and reassuring…' I surmised.

I wished to say, "Please leave me alone. I won't linger here for a long time, I promise," But I could not utter a word. Instead touched my dry lips with my tongue to moisten them. I could feel his grip becoming brutally tight. It did not demonstrate a promise to safeguard me but rather a repulsive shade of possessiveness of a tyrant.

I sleepily changed sides in the bed. I could hear the sound of anklet bells and a dafli. Somebody was knocking at the outer gate with a stick. Who could it be? ...Oh yes... Since last week, the month of Ramzan and the roza's have begun, I mused to myself.

"Be quick. Haven't you heard the fakir's reciting at our gate? You need to cook, and we all need to finish our meals before sunrise. Yesterday evening we had guests, and there is no ready food for the meals. You had decided to make roties and pakode. Get up," Ahmad whispered audibly just to me, trying to wake me up. That made me get up from my dreamy sleep.

Shabnam and Shakil were fast asleep; he did not want to disturb them. I held his palm and placed it on my chest. He placed his leg on mine and patted me lightly. Normally, I would have been more than happy and secure by such an action, but not today, after that horrifying dream. Yet, I patted him with false emotions, pretending to be a caring and loving wife. That reminded me of our pet dog Tiger. Whenever we pat him with affection, he palpably feels elated. I noticed a similar reaction from Ahmad. I was surprised by my falsity and felt guilty too.

This man had given me everything in life. My Mom was deeply shocked when she had heard about our affair. She had used all tactics to dissuade me from marrying him. She had made me sit in front of the altar where the idol of Lord Shiva was placed and promise that I would never see him in my life. In spite of all those efforts, I could not control my infatuation for him. There was nothing amiss in Ahmad except that he did not belong to our religion. Everything else was acceptable. Unfortunately one day somebody had exposed me and informed about our meetings. Dada, my elder brother, was mad with rage. Mom panicked and started hitting her head on the wall. Dad tried to dissuade me with helpless pleas. I could never understand why these people were so concerned with his being a Muslim. Though Hindu by religion, we were not a ritual-bound Hindu family. We weren't religious-minded people. All of a sudden, why this love for Hinduism? I could never fathom.

"These people are ruthless. Do not come to us when he would treat you with inhuman cruelty," were the words uttered by Mom as if like a curse. That did not deter me from eloping from home. Yet her words kept echoing in my mind, haunting me for quite a long time.

It was only the blind faith in Ahmad's love and integrity that I could take this bold step to leave my parents' home and break all the earlier blood relations. That time it was not easy for me to cope up with the new life. I was scared to death, helpless, and Ahmad had understood me in every possible way. He was aware that I had abandoned my people and my religion just to be with him. He had to convince his parents and urge them to accept me into the family.

How did I feel while forgoing my religion and accepting his instead? Wasn't I overwhelmed with the feeling of sacrifice I had done for my love and for him?

Despite him fulfilling all the promises made at the time of elopement: renting a small, cozy house on the outskirts of the city, purchasing a TV set, refrigerator, beds, and a folding dining table with chairs to match.. and despite the fact that nobody among our fellow Muslims has ever misbehaved with me, and that at times, he has defended me when someone tried to criticize or make fun of me, I can't shake the feeling that something is wrong. On my insistence, he even allowed me to undergo surgery after the birth of our two kids. He made efforts to enroll them in a better school. Now, what's wrong with me? Is it because I am lonely without my near and dear ones? I have not only severed relations with my relatives but also lost contact with my friends.

I washed my mouth and started working. I took out the chicken breast from the fridge, which Ahmad had bought the previous day from Aslamchacha. In a big vessel, I mixed gram flour for the pakoda. I was amazed to see myself doing these things with deft hands without any qualms. While cutting the chicken, I was reminded of how I used to feel nauseated with just a glimpse of these things. Initially, I couldn't even tolerate the smell of non-vegetarian food, let alone handle and cook it! I had shuddered the first time I touched fish and ran to the basin to vomit. Nobody had criticized me then. Ahmad and his Ammi taught me how to cook these dishes. I used to wash my hands frequently after handling these ingredients, yet he never ridiculed me. The cooker whistle blew with a harsh noise, bringing me back to the present.

I laid the namaz mat when I heard Ahmad approaching towards me and covered my head with the chunni. We sat together for the morning namaz. I was doing everything like a machine; I could hear Ahmad breathing and muttering religious scriptures. As I sat there, I could see a beautiful idol of Lord Shiv sitting with closed eyes. I could visualize the bluish idol, like the one in the Pataleshwar temple I had been to in my dream. I could clearly see the long hair tied on the head, the smiling expression, the cobra coiled around the neck, and the tiger skin draped around his waist with a trident held in Shiva's hands. When had I observed these minute details? How come I could now visualize those?

My reverie was broken by the harsh voice of Ahmad. He was shouting at me, "What are you doing, woman?"

I looked at him. Shakil too had joined us on the mat next to Ahmad. He was looking at me with a strange expression. Ahmad was palpably annoyed with me. What had I done to enrage them? Like them, I too was muttering scriptures... Then I came to my senses and realized my mistake: I was chanting "Om" instead of the kalma from the Quran.

I slapped on both of my cheeks and admitted, "I don't know what's wrong with me these days. Sorry, it was a blunder on my part."

Ahmad was somewhat pacified by this response. Yet I was not sure he would forgive me so easily. Had he really forgiven me? He looked confused, not angry. I could not read the deeper meaning behind his confusion. Shakil too looked wrapped in his own thoughts.

I hastened to the kitchen, leaving the responsibility of tidying the namaz mat. I started frying the pakodas and served them with meat on three plates. We finished our meals without speaking to each other and again went to bed as usual.

Today, it was impossible for me to sleep again. It was destined to happen one of these days. Unknowingly, I had chanted "Om" instead of the Muslim prayer. I apologized for the same. But am I really sorry for it? Again, the same holy idol of Lord Shiva appeared before my eyes, and my heart started throbbing with excitement. Inadvertently, my eyes flooded with tears and started flowing endlessly.

I am not at all unhappy. There doesn't seem to be the slightest remorse; in fact, I am experiencing inexplicable gratification. For the last couple of weeks, I am always reminded of Lord Shiva, but this type of experience I never had in life!

I was yearning to go to the temple and offer my prayers with folded hands. I longed to listen to a devotional song describing the Gods and his devotees. I cannot understand this transformation in me. Whenever I pass the temple standing on the corner of the road, my feet refuse to proceed. I try to peep in with hope to see the idol.

For the next two days, I was cautious not to display my inner feelings. I did not wish to give Ahmad a cause to get annoyed with me by my words or actions. Yet, at the time of namaz, I could not help visualizing the idol of Lord Shiva and the holy bull in front of the idol. I could not control the yearning. Nobody could have cured me of this obsession. I was under the impression that Ahmad would not be able to see through me and my uncontrollable yearning. But I was proved wrong. He asked me one day while the kids had gone out to play with their friends.

"What's your problem? Why are you quiet nowadays? Any problem with you?" Ahmad asked.

"No. What problem could there be? Why do you ask me about it?" I replied.

"We have been married for the last eleven years. You were never so engrossed in your own thoughts. Have you seen your face in the mirror?" he argued.

I inadvertently tried to wipe out my face with bare palm as if that would have wiped the gloomy expression from my face. All these years I had no secrets from Ahmad. I was at a loss to find a way to explain my feelings without hurting his. I nodded my head hesitantly.

"Look, you are not even able to refuse my claim. At night you keep on babbling incoherently."

It didn't occur to me to get annoyed with him. I was scared and surprised. 'What was it that I was babbling during sleep? Am I chanting Om like the other day?' I mused.

"Ahmad, I don't know how to put it. You may get annoyed with me, I am afraid. Yet I will have to say this." As his aggressive stance became more and more apparent, I resorted to a tame and defensive stance.

There appeared a mixed expression on his face, suggesting anger, shock, and suspicion all at the same time. I placed my palm on his and pleaded, "Look, you are getting upset with me... I feel like visiting the Shiv temple. I yearn to chant the holy scripture. I can't suppress that yearning. What difference does it make, tell me. I do not bother you in any way. Neither do I teach our kids anything from Hinduism…"

"Now I got it. What Rasul had complained about you was, in fact, the truth. The other day he saw a woman coming out of the temple standing near Arram talkies. He claimed that she resembled you but she had worn a bindi on her forehead. Did you put on a bindi?"

"What's wrong with that? Have I ever worn a bindi in your presence? I wear a string of black beads with a golden pendant. How could I have gone in without wearing a bindi on my forehead? That's why I had to do it. Yet I did not use a red bindi, but a colored one," I pleaded with a more defensive tone.

Why was I giving these justifications to him? Was he capable of grasping them? I had never stood against his religion. In fact, like a pious Muslim, I was offering namaz five times a day and observing fasts in the month of Ramzan. If Eid happened to fall on the same day as the Ganpati festival, I had never objected to cooking meat. Not only did I cook it, but I also ate it with others. We were celebrating all his festivals in the conventional manner. One year, Eid fell on the Hartalika fast for us, Hindu girls, and yet I did not budge from cooking and consuming meat and fish. That time, my inner soul refused to eat those things. I dared not talk about our Hindu festival for fear of his anger.

"There is no question of what's wrong and what's right. What had we decided at the time of our wedding? You have abandoned your religion as per our deal. Now why this new fad? What has gone wrong with you? Have you ever had to forgo anything just because you abandoned your religion? The other day, Shakil found a photo of some Hindu God in your purse. And yesterday I found this underneath our mattress," he claimed, showing me the holy book Shivleelamrut. I could read hatred on his distorted face. I hastened to take away that holy book from his hands. He could have probably torn it or thrown it in the dustbin.

"Allah kasam, you won't tear it, okay? Please give it back to me," I urged.

His misplaced actions could have affected the fate of our entire family, but he was not aware of it. A page was torn from the book while I was struggling to retrieve it from him. It was a bad omen, and I was terrified. What's going on? What would be the consequences of this sinful act? It indicated an ill omen, I surmised. I started weeping and shivering with premonition. I could not judge whether Ahmad was more angry or more sad because of this incident.

Straightening the torn page, he handed over the holy book to me.

"According to Islam, we are prohibited from worshiping any idol. This will not be tolerated in my house. Today, the children know about your wrong deeds, they may go and tell people about it in the colony. The other day, Rasul saw you coming out of the temple; tomorrow somebody else would see you. People would tell Ammi and Abba about it. Why are you inviting trouble for us? Let us run our house smoothly and peacefully," Ahmad tried to convince me.

The words 'my house' uttered by Ahmad hurt me the most. How can the household belong to him alone? After running it for almost twelve years by me, he was declaring it to belong solely to him? I suppressed these rebellious thoughts deep down inside me. There were more urgent and serious topics to think about. Was Ahmad against my behavior, or was he afraid of the people around us? Was he scared of the community around us? At the time of elopement and wedding, he had behaved like a lion. He was not scared of anyone. Or is he just pretending to be scared? There were lots of unsolved questions. But ignoring those I confessed to him, "I am not doing it deliberately. There seems to be an unknown inner compulsion."

"You have gone crazy. I will not tolerate it," he retorted.

Many more questions sprung up in my mind. What did he mean by 'won't tolerate'? Is he going to beat me or drive me out of our house? Till this day everything went well. He won't punish me like this just because I offer prayers to Lord Shiva. Suppose he steps down to this level? Would he divorce me? I do not have a home to fall back upon. I do not have a single place in the whole world to rest my tired body except our tiny home.

The children arrived and our discussion ended there. I went inside the kitchen with my head bent down.

My mind was uncontrollable, even to myself. Despite Ahmad's anger, my mind was not prepared to give up the passionate devotion for Lord Shiva. Throughout the day and night, chanting of 'Om Namah Shivaya' continued inside me. Even I was amazed by it. How has this come my way? I did not wish to confront Ahmad, and yet the gratification achieved by the prayers was equally tempting. Arguments between us kept increasing. Ahmad knew only one remedy to put an end to it. At night on those days, he invariably needed my body.

When this happened the first time, I thought he was angry with me. He had never been so brutal in our intimate moments. Later on, I noticed that the brutality and revenging attitude gradually subsided, replaced by helplessness. I used to pity him for that. Sometimes he hugged me like a frightened kid. Sometimes he appeared to be coaxing and urging me to change my behavior through his lovemaking. In the initial period, I too used to succumb willingly to his wishes. I used to feel guilty because of the torture he had to undergo due to my unpleasant behavior, yearning for Lord Shiva. I used to try to be romantic and respond to him willingly. Probably, we considered that to be the only solution to save our marriage.

Nowadays, I could sense that the kids had become introverted and had stopped giggling and chatting. On a Monday, I was busy in the kitchen when Shabnam hugged me from behind and asked me, "Ammi. Tell me, you are not Hindu, right?"

I was astonished.

"No. I am not Hindu now... anymore," I replied. For the first time, I experienced a pang of grief while admitting the fact. But I noticed the stress on Shabnam's innocent face subsiding.

"Then why did Yasmin apa claim so?"

"Because I was Hindu before I got married to your Dad."

We ladies often say that we used to wear skirt-blouse before beginning to wear a sari. I thought my acceptance to being once Hindu was expressed in as simple a statement as that. Till this moment, I was never ashamed of being Hindu. Yet now I was ashamed of once being a Hindu and currently not being a Hindu. I could not comprehend the deep meaning of this turmoil boiling inside me. I did not wish to think further, neither did I wish to say a word about it. But there was no end to Shabnam's series of questions.

"Are Hindu people's Allah bad?" she asked innocently.

"God belonging to any religion can't be bad. That's what we are being taught since childhood," I replied.

The word 'we' had slipped unknowingly from me; but it made one thing clear to me: now there were two parties in our sweet home. My party was in the minority and weak. I was alone.

"Our teacher often tells us the same. Why is Dad annoyed with you for worshiping another Allah?" she asked further.

The answer to her question was not simple and easy. Both Ahmad and I hadn't grasped it completely, I admitted to myself.

At that very moment, Shakil entered. I was taken aback to see his appearance. Tufts of hair were astray, his face was red with rage, and the front of his shirt was full of creases. Probably he had a skirmish with one of his friends, I mused. I stepped in his direction with the intention to confirm that he was not hurt. He forcefully pushed me aside. Is he so strong? Does he nurture so much suppressed hatred for me?

I tried to talk to him, upon which he shouted loudly at me, "It's all because of you. My friends taunt and tease me."

I could guess what must have happened. Somebody must have talked along similar lines as Yasmin, I mused. Now this issue was no longer limited to me and Ahmad.

. . . .

Something needed to be done to resolve the issue, I knew. But I had never imagined that Ahmad would take me to a psychiatrist. The person who believes in the sanctity of roza in the Ramzan and getting up before sunrise to have Suhoor, has no right to question the sanctity of our religious customs and fasts. If I am crazy, he too falls in the same category. A person who can blindly believe in offering namaz five times a day cannot call me out of mind if I chant holy scriptures. His Abbu always utters the word 'Inshallah,' but I never say 'deva shapath.'

Had Ahmad taken me to any Hindu doctor, he wouldn't have labeled me as 'crazy' or psychotic. Even Ahmad must have been fully aware of it. His psychiatrist was bound to be a Muslim, I knew. All of them were conspiring against me and trying to prove me to be mad, I suspected.

To whom should I go now? I had broken all ties with my parents for the last eleven years. I have forgotten everything that belonged to my childhood. I confided in Ahmad and expressed my refusal. With a sad smile on his face, he tried to talk to me about the pertinent things. Then I knew how lonely he too was. He too was not too close to his people. The Muslim community would not have cooperated with him had he gone to them for advice. Even if anybody listened to Ahmad's concerns, they would have criticized his decision to marry a Hindu girl. Their advice and decision could have been harsh and uncompromising. Probably they would have suggested talaq.

Or they would have given a strong verdict against me. Ahmad did not want that to happen.

That's why he had decided to take me to a progressive Muslim doctor, Dr. Ali, working for 'Muslim Satyashodhak Samaj' (An organization working for the upliftment of the Muslim community). For the first time, I became fully aware of his dilemma and the things he was afraid of. I felt genuinely sorry for him. At the same time, I was relieved to know that he was not contemplating a divorce.

It would have been desirable and wiser for Ahmad to visit this doctor by himself before taking me to meet him, I thought. I had suggested the same to him. He got annoyed with me but could not look straight in my eyes. Then I realized that he was afraid of going alone to Dr. Ali. Thus we went to meet Dr. Ali with so many reservations in our minds.

His dispensary was very modest and located in a narrow lane. It was an overstatement to name that dingy place as a dispensary. Was it really a dispensary, I doubt. In which branch of medicine was he trained? The nameplate on the door said he was a 'counselor'.

The nameplate too was old and discolored. The furniture was too modest and old. Many photo frames and notices were hung on the walls of the said dispensary which informed about the 'Muslim Satyashodhak Samaj'. A few cuttings from Hindi newspapers were kept on the only centerpiece in the room. A partitioned room was meant to be a waiting room for the patients. One could hear the conversation taking place between the doctor and patient on the other side of the partition. There was a group of seven young men whispering in a mixed language. I had never visited such a shabby dispensary. I was utterly disappointed.

The whole group went inside the doctor's room to discuss something about a proposed event. Within ten minutes, they left the dispensary and we were called inside. Ahmad introduced me as 'my bibi' to him, and according to the convention, I greeted him with 'Salam Alekum,' covering my head with the chunni. He reciprocated with 'Allekum salam.' Then Ahmad started narrating our story to him, starting from our love affair during the college days. He told him how we eloped and got married in the Muslim traditional wedding after I abandoned my religion. He did not leave any minor details from Abbu-Ammi's initial reluctance and to eventual acceptance to welcome me as a daughter-in-law. He described the first decade of our married life during which we were blessed with two kids, Shakil and Shabbu. He also frankly told him about my quick transformation according to his expectations. Dr. Ali was looking at me from time to time as if for my consent to what Ahmad had to tell.

While narrating about my devotion to Lord Shiva, his style of narration changed. He was palpably ashamed, not only of me but also of himself. Especially when the doctor interjected him, asking a couple of questions, he got irritated. He had no answers to many of the questions. When unable to reply, he started throwing allegations at me. He started claiming me to be out of my mind, crazy, and mad. In case I began to reply, he signaled me to keep quiet. It became clear to me that despite arguing with him, he still had not understood my precarious condition. He had not understood my feelings and longing for eternal bliss.

If the person whom I had loved for more than a decade could not understand me, what would be the chances of a stranger like Dr. Ali believing me? A couple of times, I could read unfathomable hatred for me in his eyes. Or was it just a misconception on my part? Dr. Ali did not interject while Ahmad was bombarding with his allegations. He not even once objected to Ahmad. How can he do justice to me, I mused.

Ahmad kept harping on the same thing again and again. 'She has lost her mind,' 'has become crazy,' and 'she needs some treatment' were the phrases that kept repeating in his description. At that juncture, Dr. Ali stopped him in the middle of a sentence and raised an objection. He announced that Ahmad's time was over as he had nothing new to add, and now it was my turn to speak. He solemnly declared, "You were given enough time, and now you are not to interject while your bibi is putting forth her side before me. If you intend to add anything new, tell me so afterwards, and I will let you speak again."

Ahmad looked offended but had to keep quiet. As it is, he was tired due to incessant talking.

Dr. Ali looked at me and said in a soft voice, "Beti, now tell me everything you wish to share with me without fear. I have many Hindu friends and know many of your customs and traditions. Tell me one thing, all of a sudden what made you behave in this fashion?"

The endearing word "beti" made me at ease with him. I almost choked with a mixed feeling of love and gratitude. Nobody had called me by that word in years! It made me believe that he would at least listen to what I have to say. I started answering his question,

"I really don't know how this happened. I do not deliberately try to annoy Ahmad. Why would I do it deliberately? At my parent's house, there used to be a daily worship, but I was never involved in it, neither was I specially fond of devotional rituals. We never celebrated the festivals on a grand scale. I never imagined myself becoming passionate about devotional rituals and practices. Even for me, it came as a shock."

"Ahmad told me that after your marriage you used to offer namaz as all Muslims do. Is it right? Had anyone compelled you to do that or was it on your own will?"

"I had promised Ahmad that I would do it. Otherwise, Ammi and Abbu would not have forgiven us, he had said."

"Was it out of helplessness that you adhered to the promise?" he asked me.

I tried to recall those days. There was never a reason for Ahmad to compel me, because I did it of my own free will just to make him happy. I was deeply in love with him and was prepared to do anything to please him. I felt like sacrificing something for the sake of love. It was my notion of pure and true love. I assumed a correlation between the amount of sacrifice one makes for the spouse and the depth of love he or she has for the partner. I had misinterpreted that the greater the sacrifice, the greater the love.

I tried to explain my conviction in the matter, "No, I was under the impression that it was the surest way of proving my love for Ahmad. I never thought religion played an important role in our daily life. I never thought it would affect our daily life in any significant way."

"What was your parents' opinion about you changing the religion?" he probed.

"They did not approve of this wedding itself. They never forgave me. They broke relation with me. My grandmother fell sick when she came to know about me changing my religion. She loved me so much! At the time of her demise, I could not even go for her funeral."

"Were you deeply hurt by it?"

"In the beginning, I used to brood a lot over broken relations. But I knew that was inevitable. My Dad and uncles completely ignore me while passing by on the streets. No one from my family ever saw my kids." I was literally in tears. Till that moment, I was not aware of the intensity of grief hidden deep down inside me.

"Do you repent for changing your religion?" Dr Ali asked me.

Ahmad tried to intercept, but Dr. Ali stared at him, and that made him keep quiet.

"I can't say that. But I get a feeling that something is not right. That's it."

"Are you feeling insecure for any reason?" he asked.

"No. Ahmad takes care of me and other people around me also treat me well. We are not very rich but that's okay. I am used to frugality."

"Are you feeling guilty in any way? Do you think you have committed a sin?"

I don't know why, but somehow I could not reply to this simple question. I don't believe in the hypothesis about the existence of heaven and hell, and every person having to pay for their karma after death. Of late, I have stopped thinking about sin and virtue. I don't remember when I stopped thinking about it. Was it when I started meeting Ahmad secretly? Or was it the time when Ahmad embraced me for the first time? Or was it the occasion when I ate non-veg biryani during the Ganpati festival at home? Or… when I started meeting Ahmad in his friend's room, deceiving Grandma and others? Was it when I recklessly confronted Dada with arrogance? Or when I used the money Mom had given for college fees for our wedding? Was it when Dad pushed my younger sister in front of me and asked helplessly, 'what do you expect me to do with my second daughter, your beloved sister'?

I kept quiet; I did not wish to travel down that unpleasant memory lane. I had driven these saddening memories away long ago. Why are they bothering me now? I do not want to undergo those depressing issues once again.

"I have already told you nothing has happened to trigger it. It started without any prior intimation. I myself am surprised by this outbreak. I follow every other thing asked by Ahmad. I observe roza, offer namaz, and cook meat and fish. I never tell anything regarding the Hindu customs and beliefs to Shakil and Shabnam. But I am helpless in this one respect; I can't stop thinking about Lord Shiv." I explained hastily.

Our meeting ended there. We didn't utter a word during our return journey. Not that I was angry with him and hence avoided talking, but I was lost in my own thoughts. Ahmad did not feel it necessary to ask the reason behind my gloom. But the way he pushed hard while getting into the bus told volumes about his mood.

That day, all four of us finished the ordeal of dinner watching a boring serial on TV. Since that day, Ahmad shifted his mattress next to the children's. I could not sleep for quite a while. I kept turning and twisting restlessly in my bed. Ultimately, I fell asleep.

I was in somebody's lap. I could smell the aroma of sandalwood incense, mingled with the telltale scent of jasmine, parijatak, and rose flowers offered during the early morning worship to the idols placed on the altar. This fragrance blended with the mild smell of the burning oil lamp beside the idol. We were sitting next to the altar. Loving, tired palms were caressing and cuddling me fondly. Grandma was chanting a devotional scripture as usual while rocking me in her lap. I could feel the slight smell of her soft cotton sari. Our house was always filled with the mixed aroma of cooking food, soap, and the smoke emitting from the mud stove. Grandma started softly massaging my feet. As I held on to the end of

Grandma's sari in my tiny fingers, she tried to set the tufts of my unruly hair lingering on my forehead.

"My poor baby gets so tired," she murmured and kissed me on my forehead. I extended my palm to touch her soft, saggy stomach and closed my eyes. I felt so secure and contented in her lap! Only Grandma and I, no one else...

As the memories of the past filled my mind, I could feel the sense of warmth and security that I had once experienced. The memories of my childhood with Grandma surface, vivid and comforting, bringing a sense of peace that had long eluded me.

In that moment, I found solace, but it was fleeting. Reality came rushing back, jolting me awake from the memory. The familiarity of the room came into focus, the dimly lit interior of our home, and the unfamiliarity of my own feelings.

With a deep sigh, I opened my eyes to the darkness of the room. I glanced at the watch. It was not even five a. m. I was longing for the same dream to continue but could not sleep any more.

With a deep sigh, I opened my eyes as Shabnam snuggled up against her. She had sneaked in my bed. I touched Shabnam's stray hairs placed on her forehead and set them in the typical fashion as Grandma used to do. Shabnam placed her legs on mine. With determination in my heart, I whispered softly to myself, 'I will find my way back, one step at a time.'

A few months back, when unlike him, Ahmad used to make love in a repulsive, aggressive fashion, I used to wish to push him away. But now, I couldn't bear this physical distance. It was getting more and more difficult for me to understand my own demands. I was longing for the warmth and affection that seemed to have evaporated from our relationship.

He did not argue with me, nor did he make love to me. Our dialogue usually consisted of cursory remarks and instructions regarding routine life. Ahmad replied to my questions only with a shake of his head and a curt nod. Over the years, I was so used to his loving words and hugs that I badly missed them now.

Now a days Shakil does not talk to me when Ahmad is around, otherwise, he seems okay. He approaches me to ask about his difficulties while studying. I have noticed that he does not go out to play with his peers any more. Instead, he helps Shabnam with her studies. There was one advantage to Ahmad's behavior; I could chant the "Om" anytime I wished. I could also read the Shiv scripture during the daytime. It made me experience the feel of Grandma's presence around me!

......

Yesterday Ahmad announced that we had to go out in the evening. Though I was surprised, I dared not ask him where we were heading. When the auto took us towards Dr. Ali's clinic, I could guess our destination, but I couldn't anticipate his next course of action. Dr. Ali had neither summoned me again nor prescribed any medicine. I had forgotten about the so-called treatment and conveniently presumed that he too had forgotten it!

I could speculate from their dialogue that Ahmad had been in contact with Dr. Ali. I looked at Ahmad for confirmation, but he preferred to ignore my gaze.

Dr. Ali said, "Beti, I would like to offer you both a piece of advice. Ahmad has brought you here with the same intention. Let me tell you one thing at the outset, nothing is wrong with you. You are perfectly normal."

I was certain about it, but what about Ahmad? Would he accept this diagnosis, I mused. I glanced at him. He was looking at Dr. Ali and not at me. I did not find that hatred in his eyes, and neither did he object to Dr. Ali's statement.

"You have chosen to get into an inter-religion marriage. Both parties have to undergo a lot of difficulties in this type of marriage. Both have to adjust and accommodate to the mutual sociocultural differences."

I was a bit annoyed with Dr Ali. Probably he was advising me to change and accommodate, I presumed. I had tried to change myself in every possible way. What has Ahmad done to make our marriage successful and happy? What does he want me to do more, I rebelled inside. Why is he not advising Ahmad to change his outlook? I sacrificed everything, what about him? I accepted his beliefs and customs, but how can he expect me to forget my inborn beliefs?

"What more do you want me to do than I have already done, Doctor Sahab? What transformation has Ahmad brought in his behavior and lifestyle?" I responded rather brashly.

"There is no place for anger. You were already made aware that life wouldn't be easy, yet you did not listen to anyone at the time, do you agree? Both of you were young then, but now you are matured enough. Blaming each other is not going to solve your problem. I have talked to Ahmad about all these things, you may ask him." Dr. Ali looked at Ahmad and he nodded in affirmation.

"It's no use discussing the issue unless you both are open to what I say. Otherwise…" Dr Ali left the sentence unfinished.

"Sorry, I should not have overreacted," I apologized.

"Ahmad is worried about two things: that your changed behavior would disrupt the peace in the household, and the kids would naturally come under mixed beliefs and customs. Isn't that right, Ahmad?" Dr. Ali made Ahmad accept his statement.

"Both of you wish to stay together as husband and wife, is it a fact?" he continued.

We unanimously nodded indicating our consent.

"Ahmad, you made her promise to change her religion, and she abided by that condition. But it is not easy to change anyone's deep-rooted beliefs and one cannot cut off one's past from the present. You must have learned it by now from your own experience. If she is running your household smoothly, you have no reason to complain about her personal practices like reading scriptures and chanting

'Om'. You never gave her such an option. She has never insisted on any customs from either religion for you or your children so far. She is entitled to her beliefs and practices as much as you are to yours. Mind you, the household and family belong to both of you, not to you alone." Dr. Ali concluded."

"What about the kids? What customs would they follow in coming years?" retorted Ahmad.

"You should not impose any religious customs from either religion on them until they are mature enough to make a choice. But tell me, how do you define the grooming of children? Offering namaz or puja and observing either roza or fast do not mean everything. They need to become good and kind human beings. They should be trained and groomed to be honest, law-abiding citizens. Is that not more important? Your arguments in front of the kids are going to spoil everything. Try not to argue and fight in their presence. Would you be able to do that?" Dr. Ali countered.

I couldn't help but remember Shakil's ferocious expression, the remarks his teacher had made about his changed behavior at school, and his gloomy, grumpy demeanor. Ahmad was not prepared to vow for it. I, too, was not sure about it. One thing became clear: We were passing through a very explosive situation, and it was up to us to find a way out. The only solace was I was not alone; Dr. Ali was there to help us.

....

About the Author

Dr Anagha Keskar

Dr. Anagha Keskar, a Ph.D. in Economics, is a prolific writer with over three decades of contributions to Marathi literature. Her extensive body of work spans columns, articles, and interviews on social and contemporary topics in Marathi magazines. She has conducted over 60 interviews with a diverse array of personalities, from stage and cinema artists to industrialists, capturing a broad range of human experiences. Her editorial expertise was honed through her role as assistant editor at Stree and guest editorships for the Diwali issues of Chhatr Probodhan (2002) and Sahity Suchi (2005). She also served as Manager Research at Progressive Research Aids, specializing in socio-economic surveys. Dr. Keskar has published 12 collections of stories, 3 collections of essays, 4 novels, 2 biographies, and 2 reportage books. She has also compiled interviews with luminaries like Lata Mangeshkar and Atul Kulkarni, translated 6 English works, including Abhijit Banerjee's Good Economics for Hard Times, written 3 Hindi screenplays, and has two novels available as audiobooks. Her YouTube channel features over 20 short stories. Her literary achievements have earned her numerous awards across Maharashtra. Besides writing, she has engaged in stage performances, compering, and voluntary counseling in marital and relationship matters.

www.ingramcontent.com/pod-product-compliance
Lightning Source LLC
LaVergne TN
LVHW041931070526
838199LV00051BA/2770